Books by Michael Lister

(John Jordan Novels)
Power in the Blood
Blood of the Lamb
Flesh and Blood
The Body and the Blood
Blood Sacrifice
Rivers to Blood
Innocent Blood
Blood Money
Blood Moon
Blood Cries
Blood Oath

(Short Story Collections)
North Florida Noir
Florida Heat Wave
Delta Blues
Another Quiet Night in Desparation

(Remington James Novels)
Double Exposure
Separation Anxiety

(Merrick McKnight Novels)
Thunder Beach
A Certain Retribution

(Jimmy "Soldier" Riley Novels)
The Big Goodbye
The Big Beyond
The Big Hello
The Big Bout
The Big Blast

(Sam Michaels and Daniel Davis Series)
Burnt Offerings
Separation Anxiety

BLOOD CRIES

a John Jordan Mystery

Book 10 | The Atlanta Years Volume 2

by Michael Lister

Pulpwood Press
Panama City, FL

Inquiries should be addressed to:
Pulpwood Press
P.O. Box 35038
Panama City, FL 32412

Lister, Michael.
Blood Cries / Michael
Lister.
-----1st ed.
p. cm.

ISBN: 978-1-888146-61-5   Hardcover

ISBN: 978-1-888146-60-8   Paperback

Book Design by Adam Ake

Printed in the United States

1 3 5 7 9 10 8 6 4 2

First Edition

For my son, Travis Roberson

I'm so proud of who you are and who you're becoming, son of my heart. So glad God brought you into my life. You are such a gift to me, to the world.

"It's not flesh and blood, but heart which makes us father and son."
Frederick von Schiller

Thank You

Dawn Lister, Jill Mueller, Lou Columbus, Mike Harrison, Dayton Lister, Phillip Weeks, Michael Connelly, Adam Ake, Aaron Bearden, Dave Lloyd, Dan Finley, Tony Simmons, Emily Balazs, Travis Roberson, Micah Lister, Randy Renfroe, and LaDonna Diaz.

Chapter One

From the summer of '79 until the spring of '81, a serial killer stalked the African-American children of the city of Atlanta.

The Atlanta Child Murders, as they came to be known, was a two-year nightmare the city couldn't wake itself up from.

During this terrible reign of terror, twenty-eight children, adolescents, and adults were murdered.

It began on July 21, 1979, when Edward Hope Smith went missing, and ended on May 24, 1981, when the body of twenty-seven-year-old Nathaniel Cater was fished from the Chattahoochee River.

Between these two murders, some twenty-six others were committed, as many as one a week near the end.

Of course, these weren't the only murder victims in Atlanta during the time. They weren't even the only black children to be murdered. They were the only ones who made it onto the task force's ill-advised and incomplete list.

Wayne Bertram Williams, a twenty-three-year-old music promoter, was arrested on June 21, 1981.

Just a few short months before—during a family trip to Atlanta over the last weekend of November in 1980—I had come face-to-face with Williams in the arcade of the

Omni Hotel.

He was there passing out his flyers, and I had intervened when I saw him harassing one of the other kids.

I had been obsessed with him and the case ever since.

On February 27, 1982, he was convicted of the murders of Nathaniel Cater and Jimmy Payne, two of only a few adults on the list.

He was sentenced to two consecutive life sentences.

Labeled the Atlanta Child Murderer, Williams was never charged with, tried for, or convicted of killing a single child—an irony and injustice I had never been able to get over.

Following his trial, officials claimed Williams could be linked to some twenty-five of the twenty-eight names on the list through trace evidence—specifically, green trilobal carpet fibers found in Williams's bedroom and on the victims—and closed those cases.

Those same officials claimed the murders stopped.

Officials stopped counting them.

Reporters stopped reporting them.

The world stopped watching.

The list stopped.

The murders did not.

And like Abel of old, their blood cries out—tortured, mournful, inconsolable cries I couldn't help but hear, couldn't help but be haunted by.

Chapter Two

I was sitting on an uncomfortable barstool in a dive on Memorial Drive, trying to find the sweet spot.

It was early in November of '86, less than a month since I had buried Jordan and Martin, and some four years after Wayne Williams was convicted.

The storefront bar was named Scarlet's and it was in the end of a tin-building strip mall with a cluttered video store, a passable pizza place, and a consignment shop with a meager amount of merchandise.

The bartender-owner was a middle-aged lesbian lush named Margaret.

She had of late become one of my closest companions and the nearest thing to a mother I had in Atlanta.

"What's your sweet spot?" I asked.

"I'm old and dried up," she said. "Got no sweet spot no more. But my niece . . ."

Always trying to set me up with her niece—for Margaret, all roads led to Susan Daniels. But she was wasting her breath. I wasn't interested in Susan or anyone else.

A thin forty-something woman with shoulder-length wavy brown hair and big blue eyes, Margaret looked like a former tennis pro. Nothing about her looked old or dried up.

I was only interested in finding my sweet spot in, at, or near the bottom of my next glass—the one that would cause the specters of Jordan Moore and Martin Fisher to fade.

"I didn't say *G*-spot. I said *sweet* spot."

I could hear the slightest of slurs in the words tumbling out of my mouth a little too freely. But even if I hadn't, I could tell I was drunk by the way I felt my center wasn't holding.

That thought led to a line or two of unbidden verse. *Turning and turning in the widening gyre . . . Things fall apart; the centre cannot hold.*

"Things fall apart," I said.

"Never a truer statement uttered," she said.

"'Anarchy is loosed upon the world,'" I said. "'The blood-dimmed tide is loosed, and everywhere . . . The ceremony of innocence is drowned.'"

Meeting Jordan the first time made its way into my mind.

I'm Jordan Moore, she said, extending her small, cold hand.

I smiled. Really? I'm John Jordan.

She smiled back but looked a bit embarrassed, her face and neck blushing crimson.

"Is that biblical?" Margaret asked.

"Might as well be," I said. "Yeats."

"What?"

"Who," I said. "A Mr. William Butler Yeats."

"This about that kid?" she asked.

Little Martin Fisher trying to make a layup on the rickety basketball goal at my old apartment complex shimmered like heat lighting on the night sky that was my mind.

Though I knew she was talking about Martin Fisher, her question reminded me of the one Wayne Williams asked on the night he was stopped. *This about those kids?*

"Everything is," I said. "Especially Yeats."

The joint had a new jukebox but everything in it was old, and that was just fine with me.

A moaning saxophone let me know another of my selections was coming on.

It was a live version of Seger's "Turn the Page" from the *Live Bullet* album. When the song came on, Seger and his band had just finished Van Morrison's "I've Been Working," and he was still out of breath when he said, "This is from '72 also. About being on the road. It's called 'Turn the Page.'"

On a long and lonesome highway east of Omaha . . .

The song was about something I had been as yet unable to do—turn the page—and it perfectly captured my mood.

The isolation and loneliness of a world-weary traveler being burned up by the road.

Life is the road and it had done one hell of a number on this young journeyman, whose center was no longer holding.

What was there to do but drink and listen to good music and try not to think?

"Why were you askin' an old leathery lesbian about her sweet spot?" Margaret asked.

She had waited until the song was over.

"You know that small, fleeting spot between dulled agony and oblivion, the one you can never sustain?"

"'Cause the center doesn't hold," she said.

I nodded vigorously. "Exactly. 'Cause the center doesn't hold. I'm trying to find it and hold it."

"They say there's no treading in the bottle," she said. "Only drowning."

"To drowning," I said, lifting my glass.

"To drowning," she said, raising her glass to clink

mine.

They say Margaret used not to drink the way she does now. They say it started when she lost the love of her life and business partner, Laney Mitchell.

Margaret Hart and Laney Mitchell were happy when, inspired by the combination of their names, they started a *Gone with the Wind*-themed bar called what else but Scarlett's.

The joint was admittedly a bit kitschy and touristy, but it was a happy place, owned and operated by a happy couple, frequented by customers who quickly became friends.

At least that's what they say. That was all before my time.

Now that the Mitchell was gone and there was only the Margaret, the place was dim and in disrepair, the book and movie memorabilia dingy and dust-covered, and a hint of desperation hung in the air and clung to everything and everyone who entered, but frankly, Margaret didn't give a damn.

"Fuck my liver if it can't take a joke," she said, and poured herself another.

I had another myself, as time slowly ticked along and Atlanta's missing and murdered children remained missing and murdered, and frankly, no one seemed to give a damn about that either.

Chapter Three

Later when Susan, Margaret's niece and the person solely responsible for Scarlett's doors still being opened, stormed in, Margaret looked at me and said, "Uh oh, we're in trouble now."

"What're you doin'?" Susan asked.

"My job," Margaret said. "What? I can't drink with my customers? What?"

Susan huffed and shook her head. "I'm not even talkin' about how far into the bag you are. You're serving someone underage."

Susan wasn't unattractive—or wouldn't have been if she weren't so closed and rigid.

"Him?" she said, nodding toward me.

"Me?" I asked in surprise.

"He's got one of the oldest souls I've ever met," Margaret said.

"I don't think that's what the authorities check."

"He's twenty-one," Margaret said. "Says so right there on his ID."

"Hey, it's your liquor license, your livelihood—if you can call it that. I just work here. Drink yourselves into a stupid stupor and let the world burn down around you. Up to you."

"She said *stupid stupor*," I said.

"Tell her why we drink," Margaret said.

"Why not?" I said.

"Because the center doesn't hold," she said.

"Oh, that. Yeah," I said. "It's why the world is burning down around us too. Anarchy is loosed upon the world. The blood-dimmed tide is loosed."

"Something's dimmed," Susan said. "I'll give you that."

"I was just trying to find my sweet spot. Sorry. I didn't mean to . . . I'll sober up and . . ."

"I'll pour you some coffee," Susan said.

"Thank you," I said. "Drop a wee splash of Bailey's in it, would you?"

She sighed and dropped the cup on the counter.

"I was kidding," I said. "You're not as far gone as you think I am."

"No," she said, "I'm not."

"I said *wee* because Bailey's is Irish."

"When you're sober you don't explain shit like that," she said.

The tinted glass door opened and Lonnie Baker, a thin, narrow-framed thirty-something black man with large tortoiseshell glasses and a slight mustache, walked in right on time.

His arrival signified the transition from afternoon into evening.

Lonnie Baker owned the video rental store at the other end of the strip mall, and every day at five o'clock he taped the tattered piece of paper that read "Back in Five" onto the door, locked up his shop, and came down to Scarlett's.

Every day he would sit on the same barstool. Every day Margaret would pour a shot of bourbon and place it before him. Every day he would stare it down. And every day he would eventually slide it back toward her without drinking or spilling a single drop.

Lonnie Baker was a recovering alcoholic who never missed a meeting. This daily exercise of facing down his demon was part of his ritual. He had four years sobriety. What he was doing was working for him, and he wasn't about to stop working it.

Today, like every day, Margaret clanged the bell behind the bar, which was followed by a smattering of claps and cheers from the few patrons present who, permanently or momentarily, weren't close friends with Bill W.

As Lonnie stood, the front door opened again, and to my astonishment Ida Williams ambled in.

She paused for a moment to let her eyes adjust and scan the room. When she saw me, she began making her way over, but stopped when she recognized Lonnie Baker.

The two hugged and exchanged a few words, then hugged again, and Lonnie left to reopen his video store as Miss Ida made her way over to me.

I stood.

I had had only coffee since Susan arrived, but I was still a bit unsteady on my feet, and I felt embarrassed and self-conscious for Ida to see me this way.

I started to walk toward her, but figured it best if I didn't.

We embraced when she reached me, each refusing to let go for a very long moment. Like the rest of her, Miss Ida's breasts were bountiful and she held me to them as if I were her own child—and for a while there I thought I was going to be.

In addition to being a friend and a colleague in the missing and murdered children's group, Ida had been Jordan's mother and the closest thing to a mother-in-law my young self had ever had.

"How are you, son?" she asked.

"Been better," I said. "Not gonna lie."

Jordan there again, permeating my being. Small enough to be a schoolgirl. Shy green eyes. Straight sun-streaked blond hair. Smooth, unvarnished, suntanned skin. A simple, understated, graceful beauty I found irresistible.

"What can I get you?" Margaret asked.

I shook my head. "She's not here to—"

"Jack and Coke," she said.

I looked back at Miss Ida.

"You ain't the only one what's been better, boy," she said.

I nodded and our eyes locked a moment before we both teared up and had to look away.

"Why don't y'all have a seat at the little table over there in the corner," Susan said. "I'll bring your drinks over."

We did.

"How do you know Lonnie?" I asked.

"Through his sister. She's a part of our group—or was. Her boy went missing back around the time LaMarcus did . . . back when so many were."

"What's his name? Was he on the list?"

She shook her head. "Never turned up dead or alive. Still missing. So never made that damn list. His name is Cedric. Cedric Porter."

I nodded and thought about it.

Susan brought Miss Ida's Jack and Coke, topped off my coffee, and smiled at me approvingly—whether about the coffee or talking to Miss Ida, I wasn't sure. Probably both.

Ida lifted her glass and made a toasting motion toward me without actually touching my cup. She then drank the darkish liquid the way someone who doesn't drink would—not sipping or shooting but taking a large swallow, which quickly caught up with her.

A quick intake of air, followed by a cough. Another swallow she thought would help, but didn't. Then more of the same.

"You okay?" I asked. "Want some water?"

"I'm fine. It's just been a while and they mix 'em up strong in here. I like the burn. I want it."

Susan appeared with a glass of water, set it on the table, and was gone.

"Thank you," I said, though I don't think she heard me.

"Nobody need to make a fuss over me. I'm fine."

I nodded and we were quiet a moment. "Hotel California" was playing on the jukebox. She took a sip of water—quickly, nonchalantly, as if it embarrassed her to do so.

Hollywood's not the only haunted hotel. Atlanta is. So is the world.

I thought of sitting on the swings at Trade Winds with Jordan late into the night, her wiping tears as Martin walked up. They were both so small, so frail, so vulnerable in their own way.

"'What have we, my good friend, deserv'd at the hands of fortune, that she sends us to prison hither?'" I said.

Miss Ida looked confused.

"Atlanta's a prison," I said. "Or at least a hotel that can't be checked out of. The world is one."

She shook her head. "I don't think so."

"'Why then 'tis none to you; for there is nothing either good or bad, but thinking makes it so.'"

Something Mama Monroe said joined the Hamlet and "Hotel California" mashup in my head. *We all doin' time, baby. Only question is where and how.*

"You still investigating the murders?" she asked.

I nodded. "When I'm not in school, at work, or . . ."

"Drinkin' yourself silly."

"Yeah."

"I want you to come back to the group," she said.

"You still meet?" I asked, my voice full of surprise.

"'Course we do. It's about all our kids. Always was. Not just mine."

"You don't blame me for . . . what happened?" I asked.

"No, child, I don't," she said. "No part of it was your fault."

More relief washed over me than I had experienced since it all happened.

"Will you come back?" she asked.

I shook my head. "I . . . don't think I can . . . Not yet. Not ever, maybe."

"We need you," she said. "From the look of it . . . you need us."

Chapter Four

When I woke up I sensed someone else in the room.

I rolled over to see Susan Daniels standing, staring at my Wayne Williams wall.

Instantly, his soft, eerie voice echoed through my twinging head. *What's your name, boy? Just 'cause I prefer chocolate don't mean I couldn't go for some vanilla.*

Dry mouth, dull ache in my head, I felt stiff and sluggish.

"It was dark when we came in last night," she said. "Didn't really see any of this. Probably wouldn't have stayed if I had."

One whole wall, the largest in the room, was covered with case files, maps, lists, witness statements, evidence reports, crime scene photographs, fiber and other forensic records—all of which was splattered with and connected by the scratch and scrawl of my scribblings.

The wall spoke of obsessive compulsive behavior to anyone listening. She had heard it right away. She'd had experience with it.

"You stayed here last night?" I said.

"My dad's a cop," she said, still studying the wall. "Lives in Tallahassee. Worked Bundy."

"Mine too."

"Yours too what?"

"Dad. Worked Bundy. He's the sheriff of Potter County."

"Probably know each other," she said. "He a drunk too?"

"More of teetotaler. You stayed here last night?"

"Mine's a drunk like you," she said. "Why I'm in Atlanta. Why nothing happened last night. I just didn't feel like driving all the way back home after I dropped your drunk ass off. And your bed looked too good and warm not to crawl into. I'd never get involved with a drunk or a . . . cop."

"I'm not a cop."

"Your wall argues otherwise."

"I'm a theology student."

She turned from the wall to face me for the first time. "I knew it."

"Knew what?"

"Knew there was something . . . Anyway . . . you don't have to have a badge to be a cop. And that's three strikes."

"What time is it? Three strikes?"

"Against you," she said. "Drunk. Cop. Jesus freak."

"Didn't even know I was at bat."

And I didn't ask to play ball.

"It's early," she said.

"I have class this morning."

"You need to hydrate and shower. So what's the deal?"

"With?"

"Why're you so obsessed with this case?" she said, jerking her head back toward the wall behind her.

"I had a confrontation with Wayne Williams when I was a kid."

"Oh yeah? Let's hear it."

"Family trip to Atlanta. Staying at the Omni. I was in the arcade playing Space Invaders when he came in with his flyers. He approached a scrawny kid playing KISS pinball. Kid shook his head. Didn't even look at him . . ."

Look at me, little brother, he said.

The kid didn't.

Williams laid the flyer on the glass top of the pinball machine, blocking the boy's view and causing him to lose the turn.

You heard of the Jackson Five, ain't ya? You could be like little Michael.

The boy abandoned his game and walked away with his head down.

Williams followed.

I stepped away from Space Invaders and in front of him.

Said he's not interested, I said.

Whoa, little man, he said. What's your name?

I didn't respond, just held his gaze.

Anger flashed in his face when I still refused to respond.

Just 'cause I prefer chocolate don't mean I couldn't go for some vanilla, he said.

"Wow. No wonder you got obsessed with the case," Susan said, "but I thought it was solved years ago. Williams is in prison, right?"

"For killing two adults," I said. "Not any children."

"Give me a brief overview," she said. "Justify your obsession."

I did—the former, at least. I had no interest in doing the latter.

The victims, as James Baldwin wrote, were visibly

black and actually poor, and here's who they were—who they are and will forever be…

Chapter Five

It began in the summer of 1979, when Edward Hope Smith and Alfred Evans disappeared just four days apart. Their bodies were discovered on July 28, in a wooded area off Niskey Lake Road by a woman looking for cans.

Milton Harvey, the next victim, disappeared on September 4, while on an errand for his mother. His remains were found off Desert Road at Redwine Road on the south side by a man picking up cans.

All three victims to this point were fourteen-year-old African-American boys.

On October 21, nine-year-old Yusuf Bell became the next victim when he went to the store to buy snuff for a neighbor. A witness said she saw Yusuf getting into a blue car before he disappeared. The same witness claimed the man driving the car was Yusuf's father, John. His body was found on November 8, in the abandoned E.P. Johnson Elementary School by a former school janitor searching for a place to urinate. Yusuf was still wearing the brown cut-off shorts he was last seen wearing, though they had a piece of masking tape stuck to them. He had suffered blunt force trauma to the head, but the cause of death was strangulation.

The first female to make the list was twelve-year-old

Angel Lenair, who disappeared on March 4, 1980. She had
left her house in denim clothes around four that afternoon.
She was last seen watching TV at a friend's house. Her
body was discovered six days later in a wooded lot not far
from where she lived, in the same outfit she was last seen
in. A pair of white panties had been stuffed in her mouth
and her wrists were bound by an electrical cord. Cause of
death was ruled strangulation.

The next victim, eleven-year-old Jeffrey Mathis,
disappeared on March 11, while running an errand for his
mother. He was last seen at Star Service Station on Gordon
wearing gray jogging pants, brown shoes, and a white and
green shirt. A witness said she saw him get into a blue car
with two men. His body was found in a wooded area near
Campbellton Road, by FBI agents with trained dogs.

Eric Middlebrooks was the next young person to
go missing and be found murdered. He was last seen at his
home on May 18. He answered the phone then rushed off
on his bicycle with a hammer. Supposedly, the tool was for
repairing his bike and not to use as a weapon. His body was
found next to his bike in a rear garage of the Hope-U-Like-
It bar at 247 Flat Shoals Road. His pockets had been turned
inside out and his chest and arms had stab wounds. The
cause of death was blunt force trauma to the head.

On June 9, twelve-year-old Christopher Richardson
went missing on his way to an area swimming pool. He
was wearing blue shorts, a light blue shirt, and blue tennis
shoes. His body was found in a wooded area, in different
shorts than the ones he had last been seen in.
Two weeks later, on June 22, seven-year-old Latonya
Wilson went missing, followed the very next day by ten-
year-old Aaron Wyche.

Authorities had yet to connect the victims and there

was little cooperation between agencies or across county lines.

The obvious crisis and the indifference and ineffectiveness of the police led three of the victims' mothers—Camille Bell, Willie Mae Mathis, and Venus Taylor—to join with Reverend Earl Carroll to form the Committee to Stop Children's Murders (STOP). This group along with private investigators put pressure on authorities, and soon a task force for Atlanta's missing and murdered children was created.

The next month, two more children were murdered—Anthony Carter and Earl Lee Terrell.

Then, from August through November of that year, five more murders took place—Clifford Jones, Darron Glass, Charles Stephens, Aaron Jackson, and Patrick "Pat Man" Rogers.

The first known victim of 1981 was Lubie Geter. He disappeared on January 3, and was found on February 5.

Terry Pue, a friend of Lubie Geter, also went missing in January. An anonymous caller told the police where to find Pue's body.

Two more murders took place in February—Patrick Baltazar and Curtis Walker. Three more in March—Joseph "JoJo" Bell, Timothy Hill, and Eddie "Bubba" Duncan.

Duncan was the first adult to make the list.

Twenty-year-old "Little" Larry Rogers died in April. From this point forward all the victims were adults.

Though not found until April, Michael McIntosh went missing in March. He left his job at the Milton Avenue Foundry on March 24, and never went back. Reportedly, he was seen alive by friends and family as late as April 1. Sometime around March 25, a man who ran an import shop on Bankhead Highway said McIntosh came into his shop crying, having been badly beaten. The man gave him twelve dollars and showed him where the nearest MARTA station was.

Two other murders also took place in April—that of Larry Rogers and Jimmy Ray Payne.
The next victim, William Barrett, went missing on May 16. His body was found close to his home.

The final victim on the list was Nathaniel Cater, the twenty-seven-year-old whose body was fished out of the Chattahoochee two days after Wayne Williams was spotted near the James Jackson Parkway bridge in the middle of the night. A police team was set up on the bridge because of its proximity to the place where some of the previous victims had been found. Robert Campbell, a police recruit helping with surveillance, was beneath the bridge when he heard what he described as a big loud splash in the water and radioed the cops up top.

Williams, who had just driven across the bridge, stopped and turned and headed back across it.

He was pulled over by members of the task force in the chase car.

When asked if he knew why he'd been stopped, he responded, "This about those kids?"

"I take it you don't think he's guilty," Susan said.

"I don't think all the cases were solved," I said. "There's a difference. And it wasn't just one case. It was many. And Wayne Williams may have been responsible for some of them, but not all. The investigation and trial were so badly botched, it's hard to know. It was a very big and important case for him to be convicted the way he was for killing who he did."

"You mean two adults."

I nodded.

"You're not here for school. You're here to solve the case."

"*Cases.* And I'm here for both."

"Seems to me you're doing more drinking than investigating these days."

"These cases will do that to you," I said.

Images of me and Jordan and Martin playing house, being an actual family, flashed inside my head.

"What happened?"

I shook my head. "Don't want to talk about it."

Jordan rolling over to face me in the bed I had come to see as ours, her sweet, loving, longing smile, the quick glance at little Martin Fisher lying on the floor. The most happiness I had ever known.

"You don't have to," Susan said. "But it involved a woman. I'd bet my life on it. I can tell by the way you drink. So what's your theory?"

"About the case?" I said. "Sloppy police work. Lack of coordination. Inane, incomplete list. Political motivations. Overeagerness to assign guilt to one suspect. Questions about Williams's guilt. Unsolved homicides. Murderers walking free. Missing children still missing. An open wound that's not healing."

"For you or the city?"

"Both. Why is everything so either-or for you?"

She smiled, but then it faded as her gaze drifted off into the far distance to something I couldn't see.

"I babysat one of the victims," she said. "I guess he was a victim. Really don't know for sure."

"Really? Who?"

"Cedric Porter. His mom was young and . . . she wasn't . . . she wouldn't've won any Mother-of-the-Year competitions. She was one of Aunt Margaret's best customers. This was when I first moved up here. I was eighteen at the time. Too young to work in the bar. So I . . ."

I knew she was older than me, but until now I didn't know how much.

"What happened to Cedric?"

"He just . . . vanished. Here one minute. Gone the next. And he stayed gone. Drove Ada crazy. Kinda like you."

"Ada?"

"His mama. She says he's okay. That he just ran away. Had his reasons. Says he still calls her. She won't leave the house because of it. Just sits there like she's in prison waiting for his next call."

"What do you think?" I asked.

"That he's dead like all the rest."

"You think someone's really calling her or is she just imagining it—or making it up?"

She shrugged. "There have been people around when the phone rang, and she sounded like she was talking to her son. She swears it's him, that she knows his voice and that he knows things only Cedric would, but . . . it's not him. It can't be."

Chapter Six

Safe Haven wasn't safe and never had been, and now it was haunted.

I hadn't been back since the day Brandon Wright's body had been found and the place closed down.

The abandoned daycare center on Flat Shoals Road just down from Chapel Hill Harvester Church, where I occasionally attended and went to school, was in Ida Williams's converted home—the very home her son, LaMarcus, had been abducted from and murdered. And that was just one of the many very bad things that had happened here.

What was once a large front yard, and then a playground, was now a sad, tragic space where rusting, slanting swings squeaked eerily as they moved in the wind, and sandboxes surrounded by litter and tarnished toys were weed filled, splintering and splitting, spilling their sand out onto the grassless ground around them.

I parked near the handful of other cars in the circular driveway, got out, and walked in.

Haltingly making my way up the covered sidewalk, I could hear the echoes of children running, climbing, swinging, jumping, playing, talking, laughing, each and every one unaware how close a killer of children was to them.

Pausing at the bench where Jordan and I had sat together on that first morning, I reached out as if to touch it, as if to make contact with an actual, tangible object that had made contact with her, but stopped short.

This was where I first met Jordan, where we had spent so much time together, where we had fallen in love— sharing cookies from Willie's German Bakery, sneaking glances, stealing kisses.

Even more unsteadily than before, I continued walking.

Miss Ida had joined STOP before her son was taken.

She and others had continued meeting even after Wayne Williams was sentenced. They gathered to discuss the cases and what might still be done in an attempt to find some sort of justice.

Eventually, the group dwindled down to just a handful of mostly old, bored people with time and not much else.

After Brandon had been killed here and Safe Haven closed, the group stopped meeting for a while.

The first time I attended the small gathering in the back corner of Safe Haven, the group included Miss Ida, a large black man named Melvin Pryor, a tall, thin woman named Rose Lee, a squat, muscular, fireplug of a man named Preston Mailer, and Miss Ida's stepdaughter Jordan Moore.

Mailer was a retired cop. Melvin was a retired mail carrier. Miss Ida and Jordan had operated Safe Haven, and I had no idea what Rose Lee did.

This time, as I passed through the dusty, disheveled daycare, where everything still lay where it was left when the place was evacuated, I could see the group had added a few new faces to replace the ones it had lost.

Safe Haven was not just the sacred place where I fell in love, but the profane place where my world fell apart.

I had truly believed I would never be back.

The three new members were introduced. The first was a shy young reporter working on a book about the case. He was a white guy in his late twenties with glasses and a touch of red in his neatly trimmed beard. The second was a skinny thirty-something African-American woman with the Free Wayne Williams Project. Odd and awkward, she seemed to lack the social skills even for a group as small and laid-back as this one. The last was by far the most interesting—a forty-something blond-haired, brown-eyed psychic with the youthful bearing and body of a teenager, a casual, unassuming kindness, and a gentle, maternal nature that made me want her to hug me.

The reporter, Mickey Davis, began by assuring everyone that everything said was off the record, that he was only here for background for his book.

"I've got somethin' to say," Melvin Pryor said. "I started not to come tonight, but I thought I owed it to the group to explain why I won't be back. I don't understand why we doin' this no more. Nobody's gonna do anything— not the cops, the FBI, the DA, nobody. Nobody cares. They've moved on. And I just don't see the use of what we're doin' here anymore. Sorry, but I don't. So . . . this will be my last meeting."

"I'm very sorry to hear that," Ida said, "but I understand. No one understands futility and frustration like we do."

"You're quitting?" Rose Lee said. "After all we done been through. How can you just . . ."

"What good we doin'?" Melvin said.

"We found out who killed Miss Ida's boy," Rose Lee

said.

"*We* didn't. *He* did," Melvin said, nodding toward me.

"We helped," Rose Lee said, then looking at me, added, "Didn't we?"

I nodded.

"It's gettin' embarrassin'," Melvin said. "Bunch of old people meetin', talkin'. Not doin' shit."

"Why *do* you keep meeting?" Mickey Davis asked. "How long do you plan to? What do you hope to accomplish at this point?"

"'Cause somebody should," Ida said. "'Cause who else goin' to? Even if we don't do nothin' but not forget."

"So you're like a memorial group," Davis said, "a—"

Mailer cut him off. "Not just. We're tryin' to . . . By sharing information, by going over everything over and over again . . . we might just . . . uncover something new . . . make a connection that hasn't been made before."

"So you're still tryin' to solve the case?" Davis said.

"*Cases*," I said. "It's not just one."

Summer Grantham, the quiet psychic who had been gazing at me with concentrated intensity, nodded enthusiastically.

"So you don't think Wayne Williams is responsible for all the victims he's said to have killed?" Davis said.

"Wayne Williams," Annie Bowers, the thin black woman with the Free Wayne Williams Project said, "was a scapegoat. The city was set to explode. The leaders knew if the Klan or a white man was arrested, what Sherman did to the city would be nothing compared to the fire set off by revealing those responsible for killing our kids."

"I know some people believe that," Davis said, "but the investigation into the Klan didn't turn up anything— and it was thorough. Do you all believe that it was—"

"We don't all believe anything," Ida said. "It's an

open group for the exchange of ideas and information. This is Ms. Bowers first time attending. Her views are her own. No one else's."

He nodded.

I could feel myself beginning to panic. I needed to get out now.

"I'd like to say how happy I am to have John back in the group," Ida added. "He's got a really good mind for this kind of thing, and his investigation into the case—cases—is exhaustive and ongoing. I'd like to hear from him tonight. What are you working on John?"

"Connections," I said. "I'm starting over. Going through everything again, anew, looking for connections—between the suspects, the witnesses, the victims—where they lived, where they were abducted, where they were found. I'm looking for patterns, coincidences, connections."

"Everything's connected," Summer Grantham observed. They were her only words during the entire meeting.

"Maybe we could all work on finding connections between now and our next meeting," Ida said. "That could be our focus. No tellin' what we might come up with."

"There's something else," I said. "Something I could really use some help with too."

"What's that?"

"I've had a blind spot—so stupid on my part. The task force's case was the Atlanta missing and murdered children case, but I've only focused on the murdered victims. What about the missing? I'm about to double down on my efforts to find out who went missing and see who still is. And I could really use some help."

"I've got a list," Mailer said. "It's incomplete, but it's a place to start."

"Excellent."

"Darron Glass was never found," Melvin said. "Went missing on September 14, 1980. Still hasn't been found. Both his parents were dead. He was a ward of the state. Streetwise but immature."

"That's great, Melvin," Ida said. "What a memory you have. We really need you for this. I wish you would reconsider leaving our group."

"I'm also very interested in Cedric Porter," I said.

"His mom was a member of our group," Rose Lee said. "Stopped coming when he started calling. Now she won't leave the house for fear she'll miss his call."

"I'd like to talk to her," I said. "And—"

"We could have our next meeting at her house," Ida said. "She's offered before. Said she couldn't come to the meetin' but if we wanted to bring the meeting to her, she'd still like to participate."

"Then it's settled," Rose Lee said. "Next meeting at Ada Baker's house with a focus on connections and missing children."

Chapter Seven

As the others ambled out toward their cars, I hung back, lingering, until they reached the parking lot, then I sat on the bench Jordan and I had first sat on together.

I missed her so much, ached for her in ways I never had for anyone.

Memories of her and Martin and our time together swirled around me, and for a moment I could actually feel their presence here with me. The grief was overwhelming.

And then Summer Grantham suddenly appeared before me.

"You okay?" she asked.

I nodded.

"Sorry to intrude. I was just worried about you."

I stood, but didn't make a move toward my car.

"Not ready to go home, are you?"

I shook my head.

"Me either. Wanna go somewhere?"

"I know a great little bar," I said.

"I was thinking this little all-night diner I know."

I thought about it.

"I can sense how strongly you want a drink," she said. "Please come with me to the diner instead. Coffee and conversation. It'd do you so good. I promise. We could even share a waffle."

"People are expecting me," I said. "I should probably—"

"Please," she said. "Tell yourself you can always drink later."

I nodded and smiled—and told myself that very thing.

"I'll drive," she said.

She led me to a beige '68 Volkswagen Beetle like the one Ted Bundy had driven. As I got in, I glanced in the backseat for crutches, plaster casts, and crowbars.

To my surprise, the car was clean and uncluttered, though I wasn't clear on why I thought it wouldn't be.

Still relatively new to Atlanta, there was much about it I was unaware of and unfamiliar with. She drove down dark, winding roads, most of them rural, none of them seeming to lead anywhere.

There was something hypnotic about Summer, and everything associated with her and our journey had a dreamlike quality to it. There was no traffic on the back roads, only our dim headlights hewing out a small oblong cave we could drive toward but never into.

It felt as if not only the road but the earth was empty.

The windows were down, the car noisy with wind. We rode in silence, as if knowing any words uttered into the airy whirlwind swirling around us would be lost, never arriving at their intended destination.

Eventually, we came out on a side street off of a bigger busier thoroughfare and into the back parking lot of a diner that could have been designed by Edward Hopper.

The mostly empty diner, which was all jade green and cherrywood, had that hushed middle-of-the-night quiet that had a hypnotic quality all its own.

We had coffee and conversation, and, as promised, a waffle.

There were only three other patrons in the place—an old lady with a library book dozing more than reading, and a middle-aged bohemian couple whose comfortable companionship and easy conversation indicated they had been together quite a while. Of course, like me and Summer, they could have just met.

"I sense such deep sadness in you," she said.

"I could say the same about you," I said. "And I'm not a psychic."

"I'm not a psychic—whatever that is. I just get impressions. And I have the run-of-the-mill sadness most every human does, maybe a touch more, but you . . . you have a deep, dark, overwhelming sadness. And it's got guilt coiled around it."

I nodded.

"It's to do with the case—at least partially, but I can't figure out how exactly. Why is someone like you so interested in the Atlanta Child Murders? What is your connection?"

"What is yours?" I asked.

"I go where I'm led," she said. "I know how that must sound, but . . . it's the only answer I have. You know what I'm talking about. I can tell you do. You're feeling your way through life, being led by . . . call it God, your guts, intuition."

I shrugged. "I guess."

"Everyone has it. Not everyone is sensitive to it—to that still, small voice. Not everyone honors it, really listens to it, trusts it, develops it."

"But what you're claiming to do is more than what your average run-of-the-mill intuition every human has."

"Not really. And I see what you did there—repeating my run-of-the-mill sadness thing. I like it. You're very empathic."

"It wasn't empathy. It was humor—a little light teasing."

"But you have to be tuned in to people to pick up on things like that. That's all I meant."

"But you claim to have a gift—something beyond what everyone else has."

"Everyone has gifts. This is mine. I don't claim anything about myself or my gift, but neither do I apologize."

"I'm not asking you to."

"You're so open in some ways, so closed in others."

"So how does it work for you, your gift? Do you see visions? Hear voices? What?"

"Hear voices? Really? Maybe I was wrong about you."

"Sorry," I said. "I'm being an . . . I need a drink."

"Maybe you need to talk about why you're hurting so much, what you're so angry about."

"I'm sure I do, but for now let's stick with how you operate in your gift."

"Ooh, I like that. *Operate in your gift.* That is what we do, isn't it? It's just on loan to us. We use it or we don't. We operate in it or let it lie dormant. I get impressions. Mostly images. Sometimes words. Very occasionally I'll hear something. I just pick up on stuff in the air. Sense it. Feel it. Try to respond to it. There are these pockets of energy all around us. We can walk toward them or away from them. I try to walk toward them when I can."

"Like with this case."

"Like with this case."

"So what have you picked up so far?"

"Pain. Brokenness. Disquiet and unrest. There's an unresolved quality attached to everything."

"That's all pretty vague, general stuff."

"I was just getting started, but I can only tell you what I sense. I can't make it convincing for you."

"Sorry. Please go on."

"Guilt. An enormous amount of guilt. Rage restrained. Caged. Sex. Sexual . . . acts, sexual . . . Some of it's just sex, but some of it's violent, angry, brutal, forced. Death. Sex with the dead. Children still in jeopardy, so vulnerable, so truly helpless. A sick, sick man, trying not to do it again. A truly evil man, soulless, pitiless, without remorse, without any humanity. Dangerous. Not just for kids. For you too."

She came out of the trance she had been in and looked at me, her deep, dark eyes delving into mine. "You're in danger," she said. "Your . . . drinking makes you vulnerable. Your sadness makes you vulnerable. Your . . . how closed you are right now makes you more vulnerable to . . . It keeps you from perceiving things, threats, motives—help and harm."

I nodded.

"You don't believe me, do you?" she said.

"Actually, I do."

Chapter Eight

The next morning I actually managed to make it to class—something all too rare these days.

Earl Paulk Institute was a ministerial college started by and connected to Chapel Hill Harvester Church—a racially integrated mega church in South Dekalb County that combined aspects of traditional liturgy with certain aspects of the Charismatic movement.

I had discovered the school and the church as a senior in high school while researching the Atlanta Child Murders. Someone claiming to be the killer had contacted Bishop Paulk and asked to meet with him. Ultimately, the meeting never happened, but that connection to the case and the opportunity to study theology and ministry had led me here.

Some of the many pastors and support staff of the eight-thousand-member church served as the professors in the college.

I had biblical Hebrew and New Testament studies with Dan Rhodes, biblical Greek with Jim Oborne, math with Lesley Ferguson, and public speaking with Don Ross.

In speech class, I sat beside LaDonna Paulk, the daughter of the founding pastors of the church, and someone I had taken out a few times.

As usual, she was dressed up—long black pencil skirt, silk stockings, and black pointed toe mules. LaDonna, like her family and most of the staff, wore her Sunday best nearly every day of the week.

Beneath the table, LaDonna had her legs crossed and had slipped the heel of her front shoe partially off and was dangling it out in front of her as we waited for class to start.

As was his custom, Don Ross, a dwarf with a flair for the dramatic and a great speech professor, said a prayer to begin class. Everyone bowed their heads, reverently, earnestly, solemnly. We were serious Bible students after all. As everyone else was praying, I slid my leg over and kicked the heel of LaDonna's dangling shoe. When the shoe hit the floor, I pulled it over to me and picked it up. Hiding it in my coat, I secretly dropped it in the trash can when I went up to give my speech.

When I finished my speech and it was LaDonna's turn to give hers, she limped to the front of the room on one heel and one stockinged tiptoe and removed her other shoe from the trash as the class looked on in bewilderment.

"I'm not even gonna try to explain," she said, then gave a great speech.

After class, LaDonna said, "You got a minute?"

"Sure."

We remained in the classroom after everyone else was gone.

"I'm worried about you," she said.

"Because of the shoe thing? That was just—"

"No," she said. "That was funny. I mean how much class you're missing, how often I smell alcohol on your breath—first thing in the morning. I mean how down you seem. You have some of the saddest eyes I've ever seen."

"Sorry," I said.

"Sorry? For what?"

I shrugged.

"I'm not getting onto you. I'm worried about you."

"I know. But I *am* sorry. In general. I'm sorry I'm not doing better. I'm sorry this is the best I can do at the moment."

"What can I do?" she said.

"There's always the sweet oblivion of sex," I said.

Her reaction was one of surprise but not outrage. She got the humor and the harmlessness of the statement and handled it gracefully—particularly since people didn't talk like this to her.

"That statement . . ." she said.

"Yeah?"

"Along with the shoe thing. Let's me know you're going to be okay."

"I'm glad you think so," I said. "I'm not so sure."

I met Frank Morgan for lunch at the food court in South Dekalb Mall.

We had Chick-fil-A and Orange Juliuses and talked about murder.

"Been worried about you," he said. "Was glad to get your call. Should've known it was for information on a case."

"It was for the pleasure of your company," I said. "Case info is only an added bonus."

"Right."

We ate in silence for a few moments.

Frank Morgan was a family friend. He had been involved in the original Atlanta Child Murders investigation and then on the task force. He was an honorable, decent man, a straitlaced straightedge who gave cops a good name, so square he was cool.

He had been better to me than anybody since I had been in Atlanta, and had become a kind of father figure since my relationship with my dad had become so strained.

"How are you?" he said. "Seriously."

"I've been better. Not gonna lie."

"Here's the question. Do you believe you'll be better again?"

"Not particularly, no."

He nodded slowly, and looked as if I had confirmed something for him.

"How about you?" I said. "How are you?"

He shrugged. "I'm okay. Always tired. Not enough time in the day. Too many bills. Wife wants more."

"Of?"

"Everything. Me. Money. Things. Time. Most days I'm a rat on a wheel."

"Sorry," I said.

"It's life. Whatcha gonna do? Thanks for asking."

"Sorry I haven't more."

"You kiddin'? You're the only one who ever does."

We held each other's gaze a moment, then nodded, then looked away, a little embarrassed.

We ate some more—just to be doing something.

A few students from the college came in, secured food, and sat at a table across the way. I waved.

"Think they think I'm your sugar daddy?" Frank asked.

"You did buy my lunch, but parole officer's more likely."

He nodded and smiled.

We were silent a moment, and I could tell he was working his way up to telling me something.

"What is it?" I asked.

"Not gonna be easy to hear," he said. "Need you to prepare yourself for . . . some bad news."

"I've already had the worst," I said. "Promise this will pale in comparison."

"Martin Fisher's mother," he said.

Martin Fisher, who had been like a son to me in many ways, was a speech-impaired latchkey kid who had latched on to me while were both living at Trade Winds. I had found him dead in my room less than a month ago.

"She's been pressing for charges to be brought against you," he said. "Claiming all sorts of horrible things about you."

Simultaneously, my stomach soured and tears stung my eyes.

"I've been keeping it from you," he said. "Trying to let you heal up—and because I knew nothing would come of it. I was making sure of that. But . . ."

"But what?" I said. "Charges are being filed after all?"

"No. But when she found out they weren't, she went out and found herself a lawyer. She plans to bring a civil suit against you."

"What's she gonna take? My VCR?"

"I'm working on it," he said. "But I need you to do something for me. Stay way from the mom. Keep clear of Trade Winds. Don't say or do anything about the case. And don't visit Martin's grave. Can you do that?"

I nodded.

"We'll get it straightened out. I promise. Just be smart and lay low. Let me take care of it."

"Thank you, Frank. I . . . really . . . Thank you."

"Sorry to be the one to break such bad news," he said. "Ruined your lunch, didn't I?"

"It's okay."

"You wanna just forget about Cedric Porter?" he said.

"Whatta you think?"

He smiled, and sliding the file folder beside him across the table to me said, "Cedric Porter. Didn't make the list because he never went from missing to murdered."

"But Darron Glass did," I said.

"Don't get me started on that damn list. Why Glass and not Porter? I have not a clue."

I nodded and opened the folder.

"You know in most missing kids cases—especially those who don't turn up—a family member took them. I'm not saying Cedric isn't one of Williams's that wasn't found, just that it's more likely a family member saw what a shitty mom he had and tried to give him a better life."

"'Isn't it pretty to think so?'"

"What's that? I know that one. I've read it."

"Last line of *The Sun Also Rises*," I said.

"Right. Hemingway. I should've gotten that one. Thing is . . . we looked at all the family. The mother . . . what's her name? Ada? And the brother, guy who has the video store . . . Lonnie. They both passed a polygraph. Had nothing to do with the kid's disappearance. The father, Cedric Porter, Sr., wasn't as cooperative. Wasn't in the picture. He and Ada never married, never lived together. I'm not sure they were ever really together for any length of time. Maybe only long enough to . . . conceive Cedric. He wouldn't agree to take a polygraph, but we looked at him pretty hard and never turned up anything."

Ada and Lonnie passing the polygraphs made me recall how Wayne Williams had failed not one but multiple.

"The mom claims he still calls her," I said.

"Really? Maybe he does. Doesn't say where he is or

why he left?"

"From what I've been told just that's he's okay but can't come back."

"I think that would be best-case scenario," he said. "Maybe it's true."

"Best-case occasionally is."

"Check out Mr. Optimistic."

I smiled as I checked the date Cedric went missing and tried to recall enough to compare it to the dates of the victims on the task force list.

"The timing fits," I said. "He could've been a victim of one of the Atlanta Child Murderers."

"Murderers?"

I nodded.

"Could be," he said. "You think the mom is faking the calls? Think she's crazy or hiding something?"

"I intend to find out."

"Of course you do, and I would discourage you, but it might be just the thing you need to bring you back and take your mind off all this other shit."

"Too bad Bobby Battle's not here. He'd damn sure discourage it."

"I invited him, but . . ."

"He still blame me for the death of one of his brothers in blue?"

"Him and every other cop. Do yourself a favor and don't get pulled over."

Something inside me sank—though I thought everything was already as low as it could go.

Suddenly Frank's eyes grew wide at something he was seeing over my shoulder and he said, "Oh shit."

Chapter Nine

"**W**hat is it?" I asked, turning to look.

"See that guy in the white silk outfit?"

Just outside an Afrocentric men's clothing store, a large black man in white slacks, shoes, and short-sleeved shirt stood talking to a smaller white man in all black. Unlike the unadorned white guy in black, the black man in white wore a white pimp hat with a red feather in it, an enormous gold chain, and leaned a little on a red-handled wooden cane.

"Yeah?"

"That's Tyrone Jedediah Johnson."

"He looks like a Tyrone Jedediah Johnson."

"He's got like sixteen warrants for fraud and theft. I've been looking for him for a while. He's a possible witness in another case I'm working. If I can get him to testify, I'll help him out with some of his warrants."

"But not all sixteen."

He nodded. "Not all sixteen."

He unclipped his radio from his belt and handed it to me. "I can't imagine ol' Tyrone Jedediah Johnson not wanting to talk to me, but if my, ah, conversation with Mr. Johnson goes south in any way, radio for backup."

With that he was up from the table, crossing the

food court, then out into the main corridor of the mall and approaching Tyrone.

As Frank approached, both men looked wary.

When he held up his ID, the white man in the black outfit bolted, but Tyrone, who didn't look capable of running, remained.

Since Frank had no interest in the white guy, my guess was it didn't matter that he took off. So I waited and watched.

Based on the body language, Tyrone Jedediah Johnson was apparently amenable to helping himself by helping Agent Morgan with his other cases.

The two men talked for a few moments, Frank making his case, Tyrone nodding and shrugging, only occasionally shaking his head.

Then from the opposite direction he had left, the small white man in black rushed up behind Frank and hit him hard with a sap to the back of the head. He did it on the run, jumping up a little at the last second and coming down with all the force of his movement and weight on the crown of Frank's head.

As Frank went down, I jumped up.

I ran toward the two men who were now standing over Frank looking down at him.

By the time I neared them, the smaller man was tugging at the bigger man's arm, trying to get him to leave with him, but the bigger man, who had pulled a gun and was pointing it down at Frank, was having none of it.

He was about to shoot Frank in the face.

All I had was a radio.

When I got close enough to the two men, I threw the radio like a baseball at the black man's head as hard as I could.

Because I was running and because I was not a baseball player, I missed.

As the big man moved to avoid the flying radio that wasn't going to hit him away, I lowered my shoulder and tackled the smaller man into him, all three of us falling to the ground a few feet away from Frank.

The smaller man began scrambling to get up right away, kicking at me as he did. But the bigger man was by far the more dangerous because he still had the small revolver in his hand.

Lunging, slipping, sliding, crawling, then gaining ground and lurching forward, I grabbed at the gun, but the best I could do was reach his wrists, which I latched on to with both hands and held on to.

He tried to break free of my grip, but I was able to hold on.

He tried to buck me off—and partially did, but I didn't let go of his wrist.

Then out of my peripheral vision I saw the smaller man pick up the bigger man's cane, pull it back like a baseball bat, and take aim at my head.

I ducked my chin down toward my chest and prepared for impact, but as the man began his swing, Frank kicked his legs and swept the man down. Once he was down, Frank raised his right leg and brought the heel of his shoe hard down on the man's face and at a minimum breaking his nose. The man dropped the cane and stopped moving.

Withdrawing his .45 from the holster on his belt, Frank slid up to where we were and jammed the barrel of the gun into Tyrone's temple.

Tyrone immediately stopped resisting and released his grip on the revolver.

"Shit, Tyrone," Frank said. "All you had to say was

that you didn't want to testify."

Chapter Ten

For a movie lover like me, Lonnie Baker's store, simply known as Lonnie's Video, was a special kind of magic.

Films at my fingertips.

Rows and rows of beautiful boxes with iconic images, each representing a VHS tape I could actually take home for the night, transforming my apartment into a movie theater, my bedroom and the small television into my own private screening room, as if I were a studio head instead of a college student.

The shop was dusty and disorganized, crowded and cluttered, but I barely noticed. It held more movies than any store I had ever been in—more than the smallish space was designed for. It held mostly VHS movies, but there were still a fair number of Betamax boxes mixed in.

Aging and faded boxes crammed onto shelves—often in the wrong category and covered in cat hair—meant that renting from Lonnie required a certain amount of patience and an openness to serendipity. But I didn't mind. I liked to browse, to lift each box from the shelf and read it thoroughly before returning it, right-side up this time, or keeping it, carrying it to the register to rent, then carrying it home, possessing it for a brief period—just long enough to be possessed by it.

When a young couple in the shop finally decided on which romantic comedy they were taking home with them and took it, presumably home, I was once again the sole customer perusing the shelves.

As I rounded the corner from Drama to Classics, I could feel Lonnie's gaze from behind the counter leave his book and come to rest on me.

"What's it gonna be tonight?" he asked.

"Can't decide," I said.

"Oh the tyranny of too many choices."

"I always get more than I can watch and have to check them out again."

"Moderation's not one of your strong suits, my young brother."

"Guess it's not."

From somewhere out of Comedy, Shaft, Lonnie's black Bombay cat, landed on the top of Classics and stared down at me. His sleek black coat was taut and shiny—even beneath the dim fluorescence of the shop.

"What do you have it narrowed down to?"

When I looked back over toward him, I saw Foxy Brown, his other black Bombay, crossing the counter in front of him, and I knew what was about to come next.

"Five, four, three, two . . ."

He sneezed loudly, pushed Foxy Brown off the counter, and blew his nose.

"Bless you," I said.

"Thanks."

"Tell me again why you have creatures you're allergic to roaming around the joint."

"Came with the store," he said. "Whatcha gonna do? So what all you gonna take home and not watch tonight?"

"Think I'll just go with *Casablanca*," I said.

"Again? How many times does that make?"

"A few."

"*Hundred*," he said. "I'm gonna get you your own copy. Hell, pretty soon you can just have that one."

"Why is that?"

"A Blockbuster is moving in across the street."

"A what?"

"Video rental superstore," he said. "It's a chain spreading across the country. You think I carry a lot of movies? I've got maybe twelve hundred. They carry over eight thousand. And tons of each one—'specially the new releases. Everything's computerized. Huge store with lots of room. No way I survive."

"Ah man. I'm so sorry to hear that."

"They claim to be all family friendly and shit. No porn. No unrated films. But they offered to buy me out and let me keep running it—until they realized I had closed down my back room. Used to have an adult section in the room right behind here," he said, pointing down the short hall that ran beside the counter. "They'll rent that shit—just through the mom and pop shops they buy and not their Blockbuster brand. But I closed that thing down probably five years ago. Ain't about to open it back up."

"How come?"

"Don't want to deal with the creeps it brings in. And closing it down is tied to my sobriety and Cedric's disappearance. The world changed for me back then. Can't go back to that."

I nodded. "What're you gonna do?"

"No idea. Stay here until I can't anymore. Then . . . I don't know."

"Anything I can do to help? We could get the word out, start a 'support your local video store' campaign before they even open."

"Thanks man, but it would only delay the inevitable. I've seen it happen to too many other stores. This scenario only ends one way."

He was resigned.

As we fell silent, I returned all the boxes to the shelves except for *Casablanca*, which I carried to the counter.

"Oh," he said, "a classic. Good choice. I think you might just really like this one."

He filled out the rental form, and as I signed it, he searched for the tape among the rows of brown hard plastic cases on the shelves behind him.

It was a slow, inefficient process, and watching him I felt the same hopelessness about the future of his shop as he did.

"Here you go," he said, placing the case on the countertop.

"You mentioned your nephew and I saw that you know Miss Ida," I said. "We're in a group that's trying to find out what really happened to Atlanta's missing and murdered children. We're having our next meeting at your sister's house so she can participate—and we're going to focus on Cedric and any cases similar to his. Would you mind talking to me about it?"

He thought for a long moment. "Tell you what," he said. "You go to an AA meeting with me, and I'll talk to you about it for as long as you want."

On my way back over to Scarlett's, I found little Kenny Pollard, the youngest son of Camille Pollard, the owner of the consignment shop Second Chances, playing with super hero action figures on the walkway out in front of his mom's store.

He was ten, small for his age, adorable and outgoing, and I had avoided interacting with him as much as humanly possible—not an easy feat given his extraverted little personality, the amount of time I spent in close proximity to his mom's shop, and the fact that we lived in the same apartment complex. But his older brother, Wilbur, a sullen, angry fourteen-year-old who always eyed me suspiciously, helped.

"Hey Mr. John," Kenny said, looking up at me with his big black eyes—eyes so wide, so innocent, so open, I had to look away.

"Just John," I said before I realized what I was doing.

Martin Fisher saying *Yon, Yon* echoed through my mind, and I had the urge to run.

"Hey Mr. Just John. How are you today?"

"I'm okay, Kenny," I said, glancing back at him as I tried to keep walking. "How are you?"

"Why ain't there a black Spiderman?" he asked. "Or Superman or Batman? Do you know? Why they all white?"

"They shouldn't be," I said, pausing a few feet away. "It's not right."

Looking down at him, I saw Jeffrey Mathis, Yusuf Bell, Edward Hope Smith, Eric Middlebrooks, Clifford Jones, Darron Glass, LaMarcus Williams, Martin Fisher, and so many other wide-eyed young black boys without their whole lives in front of them who haunted my dreams.

"Sure ain't. Do you like super heroes? I do. Wilbur don't so much. Says they no such thing. Who's your favorite?"

"Probably be Batman," I said.

"Mine too. How 'bout that."

Through the plate glass window, I could see Wilbur inside the shop, sitting in one of his mom's unsold old chairs. He appeared to be practicing his bored, disinterested look. But that couldn't be right. It didn't need any practice.

When he spotted us talking, he came to the door and told Kenny to come inside.

"Bye Mr. John," he said.

"Bye Kenny. You take care."

"You too now."

"Hey, you forgot one," I said, picking up a well-worn Aquaman.

"I know why Aquaman ain't black," Kenny said. "We can't swim so good."

I thought of Earl Terrell and Christopher Richardson, both boys last seen at or on their way to a public swimming pool, both bodies found in a wooded area some seventy-five feet off Redwine Road.

When Kenny started to return to get it, Wilbur grabbed him and pushed him inside. "I told you 'bout talkin' to strangers."

He then stepped over and snatched the figure from my outstretched hand.

"Listen to your brother, Kenny," I said. "Always be very careful. There are some really bad people in the world."

Chapter Eleven

I was nursing a drink at Scarlett's when Summer Grantham walked in.

The drink special tonight was called a One-in-fourteen-hundred—the number of actresses who auditioned during the search for Scarlett.

I was not having the special.

Summer, dressed in jeans, T-shirt, and Keds, looked seventeen instead of forty-seven or whatever she actually was. She stood in the doorway until she saw me, then walked over, her long blond hair fluttering in the wake of her movement.

I must have looked surprised to see her.

"Surprised to see me?" she said.

She was wearing a faded Pink Floyd *Dark Side of the Moon* T-shirt that fit her girlish figure in the same way the jeans did—as if designed to do so.

"I am," I said, standing and offering to help her onto the barstool beside mine. "How'd you find me?"

She didn't take the offer of a seat.

"I'm psychic," she said. "Well, that and I asked Miss Ida. I've been trying to get in touch with you all afternoon. Are you okay?"

"Yeah, why?"

"I just felt you were in danger earlier today. Saw a man in a white suit."

"Really?"

"But you're okay?"

"I am."

"Sometimes I'm wrong, but it seemed real. I was certain—"

"You weren't wrong," I said. "But I'm okay."

"I prayed for you."

"I'm sure it helped. Can I buy you a drink? Want to join me?"

"I can't stay. Just wanted to make sure you're okay."

"Thank you. That means a lot. Sure you can't stay?"

"Take care, John. I mean be careful."

She then leaned in, kissed me on the cheek, and was gone.

Immediately, I could see Susan making her way over to me. She had been eyeing us while we spoke, and now that Summer was gone, she was determined to come over and inquire, though she tried to be subtle about it. Tried and failed.

"Who was that?" Susan asked.

She was wearing what she always wore when waitressing here, a red halter top with white lace trim meant to resemble the top of Scarlett's dress from the movie poster, and blue jean cutoffs with a Rebel flag patch on each ass cheek.

"Summer Grantham. She's part of our group."

"She's a cutie," Margaret said from behind the bar. "Got good energy."

When she wore it, Margaret's uniform was a faux tux patterned after Rhett Butler's, but she rarely wore it anymore, and didn't have it on tonight.

"Group?" Susan said.

"Missing and murdered kids."

"You should take her out, John," Margaret said. "She'd be good for you. I can tell."

"Bit old for you, isn't she?" Susan said to me, as if only tossing it out as a casual observation.

"It's not like that."

"Looked like that to me. Looked exactly like that."

Lonnie walked in and Margaret moved away to make him the drink he wouldn't.

I expected disapproval from him, but he smiled and waved.

This time instead of just staring at the drink, he picked it up.

Maybe that's why there was no disapproval. Was he about to join us in our slow, sweet self-destruction?

He then raised the glass to me and said, "Here's lookin' at you, kid."

I lifted my glass and smiled.

Without taking so much as a sip, he returned the drink to Margaret and walked out.

"What was that about?" Susan said.

I tapped the brown tape case on the bar beside me. "*Casablanca.*"

"Again?"

"What's your nationality, John?" Margaret asked.

"I'm a drunkard."

"Makes you a citizen of the world."

We drank to that.

Chapter Twelve

In all, I drank less than I had been. A good bit less. And though Susan offered to, I was able to drive myself home.

Home was Memorial Manor, an older medium-sized apartment complex a block off Memorial Drive near the I-285 exit—and, actually, just a walk through the woods from Scarlett's, though so far I had never walked it.

As usual, my apartment was empty, my roommate at work.

Stepping into the darkness, my surroundings felt strange and unfamiliar.

We hadn't been here long, and I was still getting used to the place. The bedroom was the only space in the apartment that felt in any way like mine. And it wasn't just because the living room and kitchen were communal and very sparsely furnished. It was mainly because of how little time I spent here, and how much of that time was spent in my room—which was where I walked straight to now.

Feeling my way through the darkness, I eased across the living room and down the short hallway to the closed door on the left that opened into my room.

There was nothing nice about the apartment. I couldn't afford nice. Hell, I couldn't afford this not-nice place without a roommate. But after all that had happened,

I couldn't stay at Trade Winds and EPI's makeshift dorm apartment any longer.

I had turned to Randy Renfroe, the college's dean of students and all around helpful guy. With his help, I found this inexpensive place off Memorial Drive and Rick Baxley, a roommate who worked at night. What could be better?

Memorial Drive connected the two most significant areas of Atlanta for me. On one end, the end that represented the past, were the places where a series of missing and murdered children lived, disappeared, and were dumped. The other end, the end that held a future I knew nothing of at the time, ran into the massive, intrusive igneous quartz dome known as Stone Mountain, and the Stone Cold Killer I would one day encounter there.

I was lonely, felt more alone in this place, my supposed home, than any other, so I poured myself a drink and went to work on my wall.

I was tempted to dive in to Cedric Porter's file, but decided to wait to hear what his mother and uncle had to say before I looked at it any more.

I thought again about Memorial Drive and turned back to connections between the victims of the original case, searching for a geographic pattern on the other end of this seminal street.

I didn't have to search long.

There are many ways to look at victimology— and though the most common is probably the study of the psychological effects on the victims of crime and their experiences with the criminal justice system, I was far more interested in the ways in which the identities, geography, and behaviors of the victims may have led to or contributed to their victimization.

By focusing on the killer, the task force failed to

perceive connections among the victims. This led to the
erroneous perception of randomness in victim selection,
the belief there was an opportunistic predator roaming
the streets of Atlanta picking off those vulnerable souls
separated from the herd. But this doesn't fit with the fact
that most of the victims were described as tough, streetwise
young people able to fend for themselves—something they
had had a lot of practice doing.

Like most of the problems with the investigation,
the lack of consideration of the victims begins and ends
with the task force's inaccurate and incomplete list. The list
makes no sense. Who got on it and who was left off was
random and illogical. And its parameters kept changing—
morphing, evolving, contorting to accommodate some
victims and not others.

I began with Chet Dettlinger's map.

Chet Dettlinger was a former cop who investigated
the Atlanta missing and murdered children case with
a small group of private detectives. So thorough and
detailed was his detecting, in fact, that he was at one point
considered a suspect by the Atlanta police.

Of the many invaluable investigative actions Chet
undertook, perhaps the most helpful and revealing was the
map he made of the case.

In the summer of 1980, Dettlinger compiled the
geographical data into three points per victim on a map—
where they lived, where they went missing, and where their
bodies were found.

In doing so, he discovered something astounding.

A pattern.

A geographic pattern that revealed the Atlanta Child
Murders unfolded on or near twelve major streets that
actually link together to form a sort of misshapen boot.

So the murders weren't random after all.

The victims lived and played and went to school in close proximity to each other, and the main road connecting it all was Memorial Drive—the other end of the road I was on right now.

After plotting the points on his map, Dettlinger decided to drive the streets to see if the lines he had drawn on paper translated into a real pattern on pavement.

He and Mike Edwards, one of the private investigators helping him, started at the eastern end of Memorial Drive where Christopher Richardson, the eighth victim, lived and disappeared. Driving west on Memorial, they passed the street where a ten-year-old boy named Darron Glass lived, victim fourteen, who is still missing to this day. In two more short blocks they passed the East Lake Meadows housing project where Alfred Evans, victim two, lived. A few more blocks west they reached Moreland Avenue. If they had turned left, they would have been able to drive straight to the place where ten-year-old Aaron Wyche, the tenth victim, died in what was said to be an accidental fall. Instead, they drove on to the next alley where fourteen-year-old Eric Middlebrooks, victim seven, was found near his bicycle.

Across the expressway was the house where Eric lived and was last seen alive.

The two men continued west, and just before they reached Atlanta Fulton County Stadium and the state capitol, they could see E.P. Johnson Elementary School where the body of nine-year-old Yusuf Bell, the fourth victim, was found.

Memorial Drive ended and they made a slight left. At the next traffic light was the block from which Yusuf disappeared. In two more blocks, they took a short detour to the dumpster where nine-year-old Anthony Carter, the eleventh victim, was found stabbed to death.

Just beyond these two places was the grocery
store where Yusuf went on an errand to buy snuff for a
neighbor, and beyond the store on Georgia Avenue was
Cap'n Peg's, where JoJo Bell was employed and the place
he left from on the day he disappeared, and where Michael
McIntosh, the twenty-fourth victim, did odd jobs. It was
also where Fred Wyatt, in possession of twenty-fifth victim
Jimmy Ray Payne's prison ID, was arrested, and the address
Wayne Williams used as his business location address on his
flyers.

Within the next five blocks, Dettlinger and Edwards
passed the homes of Anthony Carter and two other
victims. In another moment they were staring at a silver
fireplug where Jeffrey Mathis, the sixth victim, disappeared.

Gordon Street then merged with and became Martin
Luther King Drive. Approaching the intersection of
Martin Luther King and Hightower Road was the first time
they had to use their turn signal. They turned right, and
off to their right, just one block away, was the apartment
where seven-year-old LaTonya Wilson, victim nine, was
kidnapped. It was also the apartment building where the
twenty-eighth victim, Nathaniel Cater, one of the two
adults Wayne Williams was convicted of killing, lived.

The two men then proceeded north on Hightower
Road to the location where Clifford Jones, the thirteenth
victim, was seen entering a laundromat and behind which
his body would later be discovered.

Then after crossing US-278, they passed the Bowen
Homes housing projects where a young boy named Curtis
Walker, the twenty-first victim, shared an apartment with
his mother and uncle.

Hightower Road broke into two streets at this
point—Jackson Parkway and Hollywood Road. They chose

Hollywood Road because it was closer to the points where Clifford Jones lived, disappeared, and was found dead.

Once on Hollywood Road, they passed the apartment where victim nineteen, Terry Pue, lived with his family. A short distance later was the small shopping center at Perry Boulevard and Hollywood Road, where the body of Clifford Jones was found.

Just before Hollywood Road ended at Bolton Road, they turned left and drove into the parking lot of a Starvin' Marvin store at Bolton Road and Jackson Parkway. Just six-tenths of a mile north on Jackson Parkway was the Jackson Parkway bridge where Wayne Williams would be pulled over after a loud splash was heard in the Chattahoochee River below.

Soon after Bolton Road dipped south and merged with Fairburn Road, they were passing the intersection of Nash Road where Milton Harvey, the third victim, lived, and just a block west was the parallel-running Kimberly Road, off of which was the entrance to the housing projects where fourteen-year-old Edward Hope Smith, the first victim, lived.

Soon they were at the intersection of Campbellton Road (Georgia 166) near the home of twelve-year-old and fifth victim Angel Lanier. Farther east along Georgia 166 were the Lakewood Fairgrounds and South Bend Park where convicted child molester John David Wilcoxen lived. South Bend Park was also where eleven-year-old Earl Lee Terrell, the twelfth victim, disappeared from the swimming pool.

Both Wilcoxen and Uncle Tom Terrell, along with Jamie Brooks, would be suspects—suspects I was convinced should have been looked at much, much more closely.

They drove on for several more miles—the longest

stretch without encountering a location pertinent to the murders. Finally they came to where Redwine Road merges with Fairborn Road. This took them within fifty feet of the remains of two other victims—Christopher Richardson, who was last seen headed for the swimming pool, and Earl Lee Terrell, who was last seen after being kicked out of one—lay in the woods close together near a cluster of large boulders.

Unbeknownst to them at the time, Dettlinger and Edwards had also driven by the locations where seven more victims—all alive that day—lived, would disappear from, or would be found dead. Their death map drive had also taken them within a block of the house of Wayne Williams.

Chapter Thirteen

The next afternoon, I attended an AA meeting with Lonnie Baker.

The meeting took place every day during lunch in the back of his video store, in the fifteen by eighteen room that had once housed his Adult titles.

Now a storage room, the walls were fronted by metal shelving filled with rental VCRs, video tapes, movie posters and other promotional materials, bulk kitty litter, paper towel rolls, office supplies, cleaning supplies and disinfectant, catalogs, clear plastic protective video box sleeves, and AA books and materials. Though mostly covered by shelves, the unpainted sheetrock walls were covered with movie posters. Behind the shelf directly in front of me were partially exposed promotional posters for *The Boy Who Could Fly* and *Top Gun.*

A circle comprised of ten folding metal chairs was in the center of the room, a coffee pot on a small wobbly wooden table between the first shelf and the door. Three men sat on the chairs, each with a paper cup of coffee in his hand.

I wasn't a coffee drinker, but evidently that didn't matter.

Like Lonnie, the other two men were black and

looked to be in their thirties. Unlike Lonnie, they were big men—one short and round, the other tall and thick everywhere including his hands.

"Hi, I'm Lonnie and I'm an addict. I want to welcome John Jordan with us today," Lonnie said. "Welcome John. We're glad you're here."

If the other two men were glad I was there I couldn't tell. Neither said anything.

"Roy, will you read the preamble for us?" Lonnie said.

"Hi, I'm Roy, and I'm an alcoholic," the large, thick man said in a deep, thick voice. "'Alcoholics Anonymous is a fellowship of men and women who share their experience, strength, and hope with each other that they may solve their common problem and help others to recover from alcoholism. The only requirement for membership is a desire to stop drinking. There are no dues or fees for AA membership; we are self-supporting through our own contributions. AA is not allied with any sect, denomination, politics, organization, or institution; does not wish to engage in any controversy, neither endorses nor opposes any causes. Our primary purpose is to stay sober and help other alcoholics to achieve sobriety.'"

I shouldn't be here, I thought. *I have no desire to stop drinking. Not really.*

"Thank you, Roy," Lonnie said. "Jerry, will you read how it works?"

"Hi, I'm Jerry, and I'm an alcoholic," the short, rotund man with large, gold glasses said. "'Rarely have we seen a person fail who has thoroughly followed our path. Those who do not recover are people who cannot or will not completely give themselves to this simple program, usually men and women who are constitutionally incapable of being honest with themselves. There are such unfortunates. They are not at fault; they seem to have been born that way. They are naturally incapable of grasping and developing a manner of living which demands rigorous honesty. Their chances are less than average. There are those, too, who suffer from grave emotional and mental disorders, but many of them do recover if they have the capacity to be honest. Our stories disclose in a general way what we used to be like, what happened, and what we are like now. If you have decided you want what we have and are willing to go to any length to get it—then you are ready to take certain steps. At some of these we balked. We thought we could find an easier, softer way. But we could not. With all the earnestness at our command, we beg of you to be fearless and thorough from the very start. Some of us have tried to hold on to our old ideas and the result was nil until we let go absolutely. Remember that we deal with alcohol—cunning, baffling, powerful! Without help it is too much for us. But there is One who has all power— that One is God. May you find Him now! Half measures availed us nothing. We stood at the turning point. We asked His protection and care with complete abandon. Here are the steps we took, which are suggested as a program of recovery:

"'We admitted we were powerless over alcohol—that our lives had become unmanageable. Came to believe that a Power greater than ourselves could restore us to sanity. Made a decision to turn our will and our lives over to the care of God as we understood Him. Made a searching and fearless moral inventory of ourselves. Admitted to God, to ourselves, and to another human being the exact nature of our wrongs. Were entirely ready to have God remove all these defects of character. Humbly asked Him to remove our shortcomings. Made a list of all persons we had harmed, and became willing to make amends to them all. Made direct amends to such people wherever possible, except when to do so would injure them or others. Continued to take personal inventory and when we were wrong promptly admitted it. Sought through prayer and meditation to improve our conscious contact with God as we understood Him, praying only for knowledge of His will for us and the power to carry that out. Having had a spiritual awakening as the result of these steps, we tried to carry this message to alcoholics, and to practice these principles in all our affairs.'"

"Thank you, Jerry," Lonnie said.

The readings were dry and stilted, the coffee lukewarm and bad, and I didn't want to be here—I didn't know if I was an alcoholic, but I did know I didn't want to stop drinking—yet there was something affecting about the paltry gathering, something true and transformative about the words being so badly read, and when we said the Serenity prayer I felt a faint stirring of something curative at my core.

"God grant me the serenity to accept the things I cannot change, the courage to change the things I can, and the wisdom to know the difference."

Chapter Fourteen

That night our nameless group met at Ada Baker's apartment.

To my surprise it was in the same complex as mine.

Like the victims and suspects of the Atlanta Child Murders, members of our group had far more connections, geographic and otherwise, than any of us had realized. Preston Mailer, the squat retired cop, lived in the apartment complex across the street. Melvin Pryor, the retired mail carrier, who was back despite quitting the group the last time we met, lived in a small house less than a mile away. But most surprising of all was the fact that the reporter and new member of the group, Mickey Davis, was seeing Kenny Pollard's mom Camille, my neighbor who owned the consignment shop next to Scarlett's, and had walked over from her apartment.

Our connections made a certain sense. Scarlett's became my bar because of its proximity to where I lived. Camille lived close to her shop. Ada used to walk to Scarlett's, and her missing son Cedric Porter, who we were here to meet about, used to walk to his uncle's video store.

There was nothing surprising in any of it, though I found Mickey Davis's involvement with Camille Pollard suspicious.

Everyone in our lives is connected by an unseen web of geography, interests, and relationships. So why didn't the task force search for the connections between Atlanta's missing and murdered children and the suspects surrounding them?

Ada Baker's apartment was clean and tidy, but everything in it, what little there was, was worn, faded, and frayed.

She was, like her brother Lonnie, slender and soft spoken with an essential sadness at her center.

"Sorry I got nothin' to offer y'all," she said, "but . . ."

"We didn't come here to eat or socialize," Ida said. "We're here to help if we can. We just appreciate you havin' us."

"Cedric ain't called in a while," she said. "He'a do that. Call every week for a while, then a few'a pass 'fore I hear from his again."

We were all sitting around the small living room, Melvin, Mailer, and Rose Lee on the couch, Ada in the recliner by the phone, Ida in the one opposite her, and the rest of us—me, Summer, Mickey, and Annie Bowers, the woman from the Free Wayne Williams Project—in wooden chairs pulled in from the dining table.

"Do you mind if we ask you some questions?" I said.

She shook her head. "Thought that why you here."

"Just wanted to make sure," I said.

"Rather than all us firing questions at you," Ida said, "I asked John to ask the questions."

Ada nodded.

"How certain are you that it's Cedric calling you?" I asked.

"Hundred percent. I know my boy, even with his voice changing, even with him growing into a man."

"How soon after he disappeared did the calls start?"

"Not long. Day or two. He knew I'd be worried the killer got him so he call soon as he could."

"Has he ever said why he ran away, where he went, why he calls but won't come back?"

"Say he wasn't safe no more. That he had to. He sorry but he had to. I tol' him his safety all I care about. Say he'a come home when he can."

I nodded.

"Would you mind taking us back through what happened the day he disappeared?" I asked.

Before she could respond, there was a knock at the door.

It was followed by Lonnie letting himself in carrying two brown paper bags of groceries.

"Sorry I'm late," he said. "I got soda and snacks."

"They's just asking about the day Cedric disappeared," Ada said.

He nodded, set the groceries down on the dining table, grabbed the remaining chair, and slid it over to join us.

"Cedric wanted to watch a video," she said. "I told him he could go straight up there and straight back."

Lonnie winced a bit, but she didn't see it.

Our eyes met and he gave me a small frown and the slightest shake of his head.

How could a mother let her eleven-year-old son walk anywhere alone when a serial killer was killing boys who looked just like him?

"I knew he'd be okay," she said. "He was smart as a tack and wise to the streets. It just a short walk through them woods. Knew Miss Margaret and Miss Pollard keep an eye on him, not let anybody bother him. Knew his uncle look out for him once he got there, but he never did. He'd done it so many times before, but . . . he didn't make it this one time."

One time is all it takes.

"And nobody saw nothin'," she said.

Somebody did, I thought.

"I was worried at first. Seen some strange ones at Miss Margaret's place, but then he called and let me know he was okay."

"Were you at Scarlett's when it happened?" I asked.

"I was gonna go, went a little later, but he couldn't wait. Wanted to get his movie and get back and watch it. So I let him go on ahead. I wasn't too far behind him."

"And you never saw him?" I asked Lonnie.

He shook his head. "Never came in. It was close to closing time. I could've already been gone or in the process of locking up, but . . . I never saw him."

I opened the file Frank Morgan had given me and glanced inside.

"I was at home when the police called me," Lonnie said. "I came back to the store. We searched all over—all the businesses inside and out, all around the building, in the woods, in the apartment complex. Ada and I were both given polygraphs. Cedric's dad refused to take one."

There was one witness statement in the file. A college kid outside behind the bar said he saw Cedric running back toward the apartments, not toward the video store.

"I see there was a witness who claimed to see him," I said.

Lonnie nodded. "Ronald Nolan. Never gave a good reason for being behind the bar, but said he saw Cedric running back toward the apartments. At first, I thought he tried my door but it was locked so he went home. But if he had he would have run into Ada on her way to Scarlett's."

Unless he was lying and didn't see him, or Ada was lying and wasn't where she said she was.

"There's something suspicious about the guy—Ronald," Lonnie said. "Something not quite right. I don't trust him. And his story kept changing. Said he was on his way to his car, but that wouldn't have taken him to the back of the building. Then he said he was smoking, but he was doing that inside. Why go outside to do it? Then he said he wanted some fresh air. None of it added up."

"But it don't matter 'cause Cedric's okay," Ada said. "That's all that matters."

Chapter Fifteen

After the meeting, Summer and I walked to Scarlett's, taking the same route Cedric had.

By car, Memorial Manor was several blocks and minutes away from the little shopping center that held Scarlett's, but by foot it was maybe a two-minute walk.

Only a small wooded area separated the back of Memorial Manor from the back of the building that housed Lonnie's Video, Peachtree Pizza, Second Chances, and Scarlett's.

It was a dark night and we walked slowly along the narrow but deeply hewn path.

"What'd you think?" I asked.

"It's so sad," she said. "Just a little supervision and . . ."

"Did you pick up anything?" I asked.

"Probably no more than you," she said. "It's obvious she's lying."

"About?"

"She wasn't just a little behind him. I don't know where she was or what she was doing or why she doesn't want to say, but . . . she wasn't on this path just a little behind Cedric."

I nodded. "Anything else?"

"That's the only deception I picked up on during the entire meeting. Everything else she said and everything else everyone else said was told truthfully."

"Does that mean she is getting calls from her son?"

"Means she genuinely believes she is."

I thought about it.

"Did being there help you pick up on anything else?"

She stopped walking and nodded.

I stopped and looked down at her.

"I've gotten shock, terror, fear, and safety. I think wherever he is, he's safe but worried."

"You believe he's alive?" I asked in surprise.

"I sense that he is."

"Really?"

She nodded and started to say something, but before she could, a dark figure stepped out of the trees to our left.

"Hey man, you spare some change so I can get somethin' to eat?"

He was an old black man with bloodshot eyes and a nappy gray beard. He wore rags and smelled so bad it burned my eyes and made them water.

"Sure," I said, taking Summer by the hand and pulling her in the direction of Scarlett's.

When we were a few steps away and I could see he was by himself, I said, "I'll be back with some food in a few minutes. You like pizza?"

"'Bout all I gets 'round here."

"What kind you like?"

"Cheese. Just cheese. And God bless you, brother."

We walked faster, me pulling Summer by the hand, glancing all around us as I did.

"See how easily someone could've stepped out of the woods and snatched Cedric?" she said.

"Or his dad could've been waiting there or . . ."

"So many scenarios," she said.

After tucking Summer safely away in Scarlett's, I walked next door to Peachtree Pizza and ordered a medium cheese.

"Just cheese?" Rand Nola, the owner, asked. He glanced up at me with icy aqua eyes from the pizza he was preparing and gave me a quick smile of large, impossibly white teeth. "No sausage, bacon, pepperoni?"

"Not tonight."

He nodded as he worked, which made what he was doing look almost like dancing.

"This for Reuben Jefferson Jackson the third?"

"Who?"

"Smelly old black guy in the woods."

"Yeah."

"His is already ready," he said. "I just haven't had a break to take it to him. Figured he'd be banging on my door any minute. 'Course, he'd have to be very hungry to do so. He doesn't like coming out of those woods. If you don't mind taking it to him, you can just go through my back door, walk about fifteen feet into the woods and yell for him. He'll come running."

Later, back at Scarlett's, Summer and I sat a table in the back corner drinking and talking. I was attempting moderation with vodka cranberries. She was sipping on a dry white wine.

"You seem to be open to my gift," she said.

I didn't understand what she meant and gave her an expression that told her so.

"I've met very few people that are, and your lot

usually alternate between burning me at the stake and trying to save my damned soul."

"My lot?"

"Religious. Christians. Ministers. I don't know."

"I don't either," I said.

She looked confused.

"I don't know," I said. "Don't know much of anything. Don't know enough to be . . . Don't have many answers, don't have a corner on the market on truth. Try to remain open."

"The irony is I'm a Christian," she said. "I just have a gift. Like my grandmother did. It's a gift from God. I don't do anything to benefit from it, don't use it in any way except to help when I can, when I'm allowed to."

I started to say something, but Margaret walked up, pulled out a chair, and joined us at the table.

"Susan, who's jealous as hell, by the way, said you wanted to talk to me. Now a good time?"

"Sure. Thanks."

Tonight, for no apparent reason, she was wearing her Rhett Butler tuxedo outfit.

"What's up?" she said.

"Wanted to ask you about the night Cedric Porter went missing."

"Figured that might be it. Don't know how much I can tell you."

"Do you remember what time Ada came in?" I said.

She shook her head. "But it was late. It was sometime after ten. It was after the video store was closed—quite a while after. Pretty sure he closes at nine. Anyway, I ain't tryin' to tell tales out of school, but— and I ain't tellin' you anything I didn't tell the cop who interviewed me—but she was in a state. Upset, distraught like. You know? And high as hell. I'm not sayin' she did anything to her kid. Hell, I don't think she did. But I know for a fact she wasn't where she said she was when he went missing."

"Anybody strange or creepy hanging out here that night? Anybody leave around the time Cedric was supposed to be outside?"

"Something like this happens and you look back and begin to get suspicious of everyone. You know? The most harmless things cause you to question and suspect and . . . Something like this changes everything and everybody. All you got to do is look at Lonnie."

"Whatta you mean?"

"He was my best customer until that night. Hasn't had a drink since then. Shit like this either drives you to drink or sobers you up. Did it to everyone involved. Made most of us drink more. Anyway, there were two guys. Again, I ain't tryin' to point the finger at anyone, and I ain't saying they did anything. Just telling you what I told the cop at the time. They felt wrong. Never seen 'em before. Never saw them again. Don't know their names or anything about them. Don't know if they were together or . . . hell, I can't even remember what they looked like. But at least one of them, and I think both, left around the time Cedric was supposed to be out there. You want more than that, I'll have to dig out the notes I wrote down that night."

"Would you please?"

"Sure."

"What about the college kid who said he saw Cedric out back? What was his name? Ronald Nolan?"

"Why don't you go ask him?"

"I'd like to."

"Out that door, hang a right, one door down."

"I don't follow."

"Peachtree Pizza," she said.

"He work there?"

"Used to," she said. "Now he owns it. He changed his name a little. A religious thing I think. Now he goes by Rand Nola."

Chapter Sixteen

"**H**e ask you for another?" Rand Nola said.

I was in Peachtree Pizza. I had come alone. Summer was still nursing her wine, waiting for me at Scarlett's.

"Huh? Oh. Reuben? No."

"He reminded you how good they are and you have to have one for yourself?"

"Yep."

"What can I get ya?"

"Medium sausage and bacon," I said.

I hadn't planned on ordering a pizza, but knew it couldn't hurt. I loved pizza and his were passable.

"It'll be my last pie of the night."

As Rand busied himself preparing my pie, I took a closer look at him. He was tall and athletic looking, with baby-fine blond hair, bright white teeth he flashed often, and aqua eyes I associated with suffering for some reason. He wore straight-legged light-colored blue jeans, leather sandals, and a pink Peachtree Pizza T-shirt.

"Okay if I talk to you while you work your magic?"

"No worries."

"I belong to a group of amateur detectives working on the disappearance of Cedric Porter, and Margaret at Scarlett's said you were the Ronald Nolan from the witness statements."

He nodded. "Changed it a couple of years back—my name. Not much, but enough. Underwent an awakening and wanted to be called something different. Wasn't trying to hide or anything."

"Didn't think you were."

"Man," he said, "that whole thing—that time, what was happening in the city, then for it to hit so close to home. Losing little Cedric like that completely rocked my world, man. I'll never get over it."

I nodded.

"It was hard enough, but then to be . . . There were people who suspected me, questioned why I was back there, didn't buy my story. It was a nightmare. To be honest, it's a big part of why I changed my name."

"I hear ya, brother," I said. "I've had a few experiences like that myself. Why don't you think they believed you?"

"Everybody suspected everybody back then anyway. It was crazy the way the city was at the time."

"Do you mind telling me what you were doing back there and what you saw?"

"Nah, man, I don't mind, but that's the thing—I've never been completely honest about why I was back there. That's the biggest reason I became a suspect."

"Okay."

"I was one hundred percent honest about what I saw, just not why I was out there."

"Why's that?"

"I couldn't be. I was with a woman—one I shouldn't've been with, or who shouldn't've been with me."

"Why can you say now?"

"Things have changed a bit. I still can't say who it

was, but I am at least willing to say that's what I left out. It was hard as hell, man. Somebody who could corroborate my statement, and I could've used 'em."

"If you still can't, it leaves you in the same position," I said. "Just makes it sound like you're changing your story again."

"I know, but . . ."

"Are you still seeing the woman?"

He shook his head. "Wasn't really then. We just got together to fuck. She was in a relationship with someone else."

"*Was?* She isn't any longer?"

He shook his head again.

"So why can't you say who she is now?"

"Her . . . who she was with is a friend of mine."

I nodded. "So what did you see?"

"Just what my statement said. Cedric, who I knew from his uncle's store next door, running toward the woods."

"Did he have anything?"

"Have anything?"

"A video? A—"

"Nah."

"Was anyone with him or chasing him?"

"No. Not that I saw. Just saw him. He ran past, then disappeared into the woods. That's all I saw. I just thought he was running back home. Didn't think anything of it at the time. 'Course I was gettin' some of the best head I ever have. Least I was until . . ."

had   "Until what?"

"Until he ran by."

"Y'all stopped then?"

"Yeah."

"Why?"

He hesitated, then shook his head. "I . . . shouldn't . . . I've said too much already."

"Could you at least ask your . . . partner from back then if she would talk to me. I'd never say anything to anyone. She'd be safe. I'd protect her identity."

"I just can't. Sorry. I would actually do that if I could, but I can't. I wish I could. I really do."

When I got back to Scarlett's, Summer, Susan, and Margaret were having an animated and inebriated discussion about God.

Aunt and niece had joined Summer at our table in the back corner, oblivious to the other patrons in the bar and the exasperated expressions being directed at them.

"Here he is," Margaret said. "Now we have an expert to ask."

I laughed at that. And not only because there were no experts, but because I was someone who had a spiritual awakening, began seeking, and had only completed one quarter of study at a new and questionable Bible school.

"What is God?" Margaret asked. "I say he's a watchmaker who made this intricate timepiece and then stepped back and is watching but not participating in what is happening. Susan says . . . What is it you said again?"

"God is our father," Susan said. "He provides for us, takes care of us, disciplines us. Involved with the world, not aloof or distant or—"

"Hey, Margaret," an older man sitting on the opposite side of the bar yelled, "can I get a drink over here?"

"Get it yourself. See how hard my damn job is. Don't mix it too strong neither, Fred, or I'll know."

"Suddenly, a fuckin' self-service bar up in here. I

could make my own drinks at home."

"Summer says God's a . . ." Margaret began but trailed off and took another slug of her drink.

"God is energy," Summer said. "In us, around us, in all things. We can ignore him or we can draw from him."

I nodded.

"Well?" Margaret said.

I raised my glass. "Malt does more than Milton can to justify God's ways to man."

We all drank to that.

"Seriously," Susan said. "Weigh in. What is God?"

"God is love . . . or . . . nothing else matters much."

Chapter Seventeen

I met Mickey Davis the next afternoon at Second Chances.

He was watching Camille Pollard's shop and her kids.

We sat at a secondhand dining table that had yet to sell, notes and case files spread out on the marred wooden tabletop between us.

The table was in between a small, faded recliner and a country-blue couch with a couple of prominent cigarette burns on it, in what constituted the sparse store's furniture section.

Opposite us, surrounded by a handful of sad toys and a couple of mismatched shelves of children's books, Kenny and Wilbur were lying on the floor working on their homework.

"I appreciate you meeting me here," Mickey said. "Camille's at a job interview. Gonna shut this place down if she gets it."

The afternoon sun shone through the plate glass windows in front and caused both his paleness and the red in his beard to be more pronounced.

"How long you two been seein' each other?"

"Only a few months," he said, avoiding my eye. "First black woman, older woman, and single mother I've dated, but so far so good."

He spoke softly and seemed a little embarrassed.
"How'd you meet?"

"Blind date set up by a mutual friend. Met at Scarlett's for a drink."

There was no obvious reason I should distrust the man, but I did. Probably because he was a reporter and the only member of the group profiting from the case, but whatever the reason, I wanted to get his thoughts about and reactions to various aspects and elements of the case without doing much in the way of reciprocating.

"What'd you think about what Ada said last night?" I asked.

He narrowed his smallish eyes and twisted his lips into a frown. "Felt wrong. Didn't add up, but I can't say why."

Waves of hostility emanated from Wilbur and wafted over us. I'd catch him staring at us in unadorned anger, but when I held his gaze, he looked away. Oblivious, Kenny continued coloring intensely.

"Is Cedric's case going into your book?" I asked.

"Only if we find out what happened to him and tie it to Williams or whoever the Atlanta Child Murderer is."

Hearing him say it aloud reminded me again that the Atlanta Child Murders were a series of murders surrounded by a much larger set of related and unrelated murders.

Don't forget that, I reminded myself. *Don't lose sight of the saplings for the forest.*

Then another thought occurred to me. *Are the adult victims on the list connected to each other the way the children are? What about the female victims?*

"Where'd you go?" Mickey said.

"Huh? Oh, sorry? Just thinking."

"Well?" he said.

"Well what?"

"Do you think Cedric could be with his dad?"

I shrugged. "Could be."

"Think we should take a closer look at him?" he asked.

I thought about all the various absentee fathers of all the various victims and how one witness claimed that Yusuf Bell got into a car with his father before he disappeared and was found murdered. I thought about how John Bell, Yusuf's dad, failed a polygraph.

I nodded. "I certainly do."

"I think so too. I'll tell you what else I think . . . I think we need to look at all the other similar missing kid cases from around the same time."

"Before and since too," I said. "If they continued after Williams went to prison . . . If they stopped . . ."

"You think all Williams's victims haven't been found?" he asked.

"I think it's likely that all the victims haven't been found—whether they belong to Williams or someone else, or Williams and someone else."

"I think it's Williams," he said. "And I'll tell you why. I found four other cases like Cedric's. I mean so similar they could be the same case. They even look like Cedric. All vanished. Never seen again. Never found a body or any evidence of any kind. It's a serial. I'd bet my life on it. And . . . it stopped when Wayne Williams was arrested."

I thought about it. If he was right . . . if Cedric was part of a pattern . . .

"The Atlanta Child Murderer didn't hide his victims," I said. "He dumped them. Most were found fairly quickly."

"I know. So if it's not Williams, it would be somebody else—a killer who went undetected during that time, a serial killer overshadowed by another serial killer. But if so why'd they stop?"

I thought of Jamie Brooks.

Of all the suspects considered besides Wayne Williams, Jamie Brooks was the strongest—at least for the murder of one of the victims attributed to Williams.

Twelve-year-old Clifford Jones, in town visiting his maternal grandmother and out looking for cans, disappeared on the afternoon of August 20, 1980.

Clifford's siblings had seen him go into the laundromat in the Hollywood Plaza Shopping Center, where, according to a nineteen-year-old boy, he was raped and killed by the manager James "Jamie" Edward Brooks, and two other men.

The boy told authorities that three men fondled Clifford, that he was crying when they removed his clothes, said, "They mess with the boy's behind, chest and legs," and one of them "got him in the butt." He went on to say that the boy was hollering really loud, saying he wanted to go home, but one of the men had a yellow rope tied around Clifford's neck, which he eventually strangled him with—a detail that matches the facts. Clifford Jones was one of the few victims on the list known to have been strangled with a rope. The witness then said the men washed the body with soap and a rag, and reclothed it.

Though all the details fit, the witness's statement was disregarded because police said the nineteen-year-old boy was retarded and would say whatever he thought they wanted him to.

When Brooks was questioned, he told police that the boy came in around 4:30 p.m. asking for a job picking up trash and sweeping, and said he stayed until about 8:30 p.m.

And that was it. He wasn't questioned further—not about Clifford or any other victims on or off the list.

Jamie Brooks would eventually be sentenced on other charges in March of 1981, the same month when the last child under seventeen would disappear during the height of the murders. He was charged with aggravated assault with intent to rape and aggravated sodomy, and would serve ten months in the Fulton County Jail and be released during the Williams trial.

Perhaps most interesting of all as it relates to the list and the case against Wayne Williams is that Clifford Jones's murder was attributed to Williams following the trial—based on matching fiber evidence. Why, if the green trilobal fibers used to connect Williams to the victims and convict him for their murders are so unique, were they found on a victim that he almost certainly didn't kill?

"Maybe like Jamie Brooks he went to prison on different charges," I said. "Maybe he moved. Or died."

He started to say something, but Camille walked in.

She was a mid-thirties African-American woman with light skin and very tired eyes. Her hair had been straightened, and it, her makeup, and clothes were stylish—or would have been a few years back.

She collapsed in one of the two free chairs around the dining table and sighed heavily.

Kenny ran over and hugged her, but Wilbur didn't even look up.

After hearing about Kenny's day and speaking to Wilbur and getting a grunt in return, Kenny rejoined Wilbur and she returned her attention to us.

"Camille, this is John Jordan, the guy I was telling you about. John, this is Camille."

"Nice to meet you," I said.

"How'd it go?" Mickey asked.

She shook her head, the long side of her asymmetrical bob waving back and forth. "Too old. Too qualified. Too late. Too bad."

"You'll find something," he said. "Just a matter of time."

"What're y'all doing?"

He told her.

"Do you remember Cedric?" I asked.

The question seemed to bother her, and she glanced over her shoulder at her boys. "Don't like talkin' about it. So close to . . . He played with Wilbur. Good, sweet kid. The kind that people looked out for 'cause his mama didn't. But I don't even like talkin' about it. Scares me to think . . ."

She turned and looked at Kenny and Wilbur again.

"Did you ever see his dad around?" I asked.

She shook her head. "I really don't want to talk about it. And I'd rather y'all not work on that stuff around me and my boys."

"Okay, baby," Mickey said. "I understand. I won't do it again."

"I'm sorry," she said, looking at me. "I'm not trying to be . . . It's just upsetting. I just can't . . ."

I nodded. "I get it. It's not a problem."

"You should talk to Miss Annie Mae Dozier. We all looked after him, but she near raised him. She moved shortly after he disappeared. Broke her heart. But I don't think she went far. I've got her new address 'round here somewhere. Always send her a Christmas card."

Chapter Eighteen

"**Y**ou killed a cop," Bobby Battle said.

"I didn't," I said. "He killed himself."

He was referring to Larry Moore, Ida's son-in-law, Jordan's husband, and one of his brothers in blue who killed himself a month back. It happened at Ida's house. I was there at the time.

"Ida was there," I added. "Her statement corroborated mine."

"*Corroborated,*" he said. "That's just how criminals talk. She's covering for you."

"DA doesn't see it that way."

"Well, that's the way me and every other cop in this town see it. And don't even get me started on a dead kid being found in your room."

We were at a truck stop off I-85 north of Atlanta, because he didn't want to be seen with me.

As usual, he was dressed like a slick TV detective, but his white cotton *Miami Vice* suit and purple silk T-shirt looked out of place in Atlanta in November.

He held up a file folder.

"I'm doin' this as a favor for Frank. 'Cause I owe him. But I'm also doin' it because of what this is for a guy like you."

I didn't say anything and he looked disappointed.

"This is rope for a guy like you," he said, flapping the folder in the wind. "I give you enough of it and you'll hang yourself."

All around us, semi-trailers and tractors pulled in, parked, refueled, pulled out. The side lot where we were was full of them.

We were standing between our two cars even though it was a cold, damp day. It was loud and hard to hear, and I wanted to get this over with as quickly as possible.

He handed me the folder.

"Copies of the four missing kids cases Frank asked for—and one he didn't because it matches."

"Thanks," I said, opening the folder and glancing through its contents.

It was thin—a few missing persons reports, a few notes from the cops involved. Not much else.

"And before you say anything, that's all there was. I copied everything."

"I appreciate it."

"Frank is welcome."

I nodded.

"I know you didn't ask what I think, but—"

"I was just about to," I said.

"Their dads took them, not so as we could prove, but that's what happened. And I'll tell you why the fine detectives who investigated these cases didn't do anything other than what they did."

I waited but he didn't say anything. Guessing he was waiting for me to ask, I said, "Why's that?"

"Because of how shitty their mothers were. Gotta figure kids would be no worse off with their sperm donors. Hell, may even be better off."

"Do you know if any of the missing boys ever called their moms to let them know they were okay?"

He shook his head. "Never heard anything like that."

"You mind if I ask the detectives who worked the cases?"

"Hell yes, I mind. Don't even think about talking to anyone else. Not that they'd talk to you, but . . . I better not hear of you talkin' to another cop."

"You won't."

"Make sure you don't. I'll ask around about it, let you know if I hear of anything like that—so don't you. Got it?"

"Got it."

"I mean it."

"I know. I appreciate this. I'm not gonna do anything you don't want me to."

"We both know that ain't true. I don't want you doin' any of this."

Chapter Nineteen

"Do you remember any of Cedric's friends?" I asked.

I had stopped by Lonnie's to rent a movie on my way home. I was looking in Drama when it occurred to me to ask him.

He shrugged. "Not sure I knew any even back then. Why?"

"Recognize any of these names? Jamal Jackson, Quentin Washington, Jaquez Anderson, Duke Ellis, or Vaughn Smith."

I didn't have the file with me, but I had studied it in the truck stop parking lot and knew the names by heart.

He thought about it.

All five boys were between the ages of ten and fourteen when they vanished during the height of the Atlanta Child Murders. None of them were ever seen again—dead or alive. All of them had lived with a single mom with suspect parenting skills.

"A few sound sort of familiar, but . . ."

I nodded and kept looking.

In the mood for something light and romantic, I was already carrying the boxes for *Sixteen Candles* and *The Man from Snowy River* around with me.

"Were they Cedric's friends?" Lonnie said. "Could

they know something to help us find him? Can I talk to them? I'll close the shop and we can go right now."

"Just looking for connections between them and Cedric."

"Why's that?"

"They disappeared during the same time period and in the same manner he did."

"Oh. Any of them ever found?"

I frowned and shook my head.

"Found any connections between them?"

"Just started looking," I said. "Just got their names and the police reports."

"How can I help?"

Settling on the two selections I had already made, I made my way up toward the counter where Lonnie stood.

"I'll let you know," I said.

"I'll do anything," he said. "I'd give anything to get him back. I just can't fathom what happened to him. And the thought of Wayne Williams or someone like him gettin' hold of that sweet boy . . . Makes me want to drink like nothin' else ever has."

"What can you tell me about Cedric's dad?"

"Cedric Sr. ain't a bad guy. Immature. Self-centered. Didn't know nothin' about being a daddy—never had one his self."

"Could he have taken Cedric?"

He shook his head. "Wouldn't want him. Wouldn't know what to do with him. And . . . He's the first place I looked back then. He was shocked Cedric was gone. I believed him when he said he didn't have him or have any idea where he was, but I still watched him for a week or so just to make sure. Followed him everywhere he went for a while. Broke into his house and looked around when he was at work. Found nothin'. He didn't take him, doesn't have him. I wish he did."

I nodded.

"You or the group want to talk to him anyway, I can set it up or even go with you if you like."

"Thanks."

"I appreciate what y'all are doing. Cops don't care. Nobody else is looking. I'll do anything I can to help. Just let me know what that is."

I sat my two selections on the counter, and he went about finding them.

"This a little light for you, ain't it?" he said.

"Need a little light in my life," I said.

"Come to another meeting with me."

"I will. I promise. It helped."

He handed me my two movies without writing them down or having me sign anything. "On the house," he said. "Enjoy."

"Thank you, Lonnie. I appreciate that."

"Just find my boy," he said, and it occurred to me that he was the closest thing to a father Cedric ever had, and Cedric was the closest thing to a son he ever had.

Chapter Twenty

I stopped in Scarlett's to talk to Susan.

It was the first time I had ever entered the establishment with no intention of drinking.

I sat at a table in the far corner and waited.

"What can I get you?" Susan said.

"Just a little conversation."

"No, seriously. Margaret said I had to serve you."

"Just came in to talk to you," I said.

"Really?"

"Really."

"Truly?"

"Truly."

She sat down across from me, placing her tray on the table next to the unlit candle between us.

"What happened?" she asked.

"Whatta you mean?"

"Why aren't you drinking?"

"I'm not *not* drinking," I said. "I'm just not drinking right now. I'm working on something."

"Cedric?"

I nodded.

It was late afternoon and Scarlett's was mostly empty. Two middle-aged men at opposite ends of the bar were staring into their drinks. Margaret, seated on a stool behind the bar, was having a moment with a drink of her own.

"That makes two of you," she said. "Cedric's death made you and Lonnie stop drinking."

My abstinence was temporary and it was because of the case, but I didn't mention it.

"Why do you say *death* instead of *disappearance*?" I asked.

She shrugged. "No reason. Nothing sinister. Just a feeling. I mean, I'm not a psychic like your girlfriend, but I get feelings too."

"How about facts?" I asked. "Got any of those or just feelings?"

"Whatta you mean?"

"You kept him. See anything? Hear anything? Anything that might help us find him?"

"Yeah, and I've been sitting on it all this time just waiting for someone to ask me in just the right way."

"Nothing that seemed fine at the time but later made you rethink it?"

"Nothing. He seemed like a good, happy kid. I didn't keep him all that much. His mom was a drunk. I don't know how bad she was to him. Think she was mostly just not there—even when she was. His uncle made sure he was taken care of. He's the one who paid me, not the mom. He's the one who made sure Cedric ate and got to school. But lots of people looked out for him."

"Like Annie Mae Dozier?"

"Her especially, but there were others."

We were quiet a moment, and I looked back over at the three lost souls at the bar.

"Do I look that sad when I'm drinking?" I asked.

"When you're drinking. When you're not."

I shook my head and forced a smile.

"What about friends his age?" I asked.

"Huh?"

"Cedric," I said. "What about friends?"

"He didn't have a lot. Played with a few kids from the apartment complex but just because they were there. Not like his mom was going to take him anywhere—no school activities, no birthday parties, nothing like that."

"Recognize any of these names?" I said. "Jamal Jackson, Quentin Washington, Jaquez Anderson, Duke Ellis, or Vaughn Smith."

"Jamal lived in the building. They played together some. Why?"

"What happened to Jamal?" I asked.

She shrugged. "He and his mom moved. Have no idea after that. Why?"

"Did you have a boyfriend during that time?"

"What does that have to do with—"

"Did you?"

"Yeah. Why?"

"Where were you the night Cedric disappeared?"

"You suspect *me*?" she asked, her voice equal parts anger and pain.

"No," I said, and it was only partially untrue.

"Then why ask?"

"Were you with Ronald Nolan?"

"The pizza guy?"

"Yeah."

"No."

"He said he was with a woman out back that night. Said she wasn't single, so . . ."

"You thought of me 'cause I'm such a whore?"

"No. It's a compliment. You're the prettiest, most desirable young woman I could come up with."

"Oh," she said, seeming placated for the moment. "It wasn't me," she said.

"It was an innocent question," I said. "Nothing behind it."

"*Oh shit*," she said, her eyes widening as if something had just occurred to her.

"What is it?"

"What if it wasn't a young woman but an older one?"

"Which?"

"The Mitchell of the Margaret and Mitchell partnership. I always suspected Laney of stepping out on Aunt Margaret. She had been with men before. Was mostly with men until she and Aunt Margaret got together. Always thought she was more bi than . . . bet she and ol' pizza boy were scratching itches they both had."

"It would explain why he couldn't reveal who it was," I said. "Why he still can't."

She nodded.

"Thank you," I said.

"Anytime."

"How did Laney die?" I asked. "I've never heard anyone say."

"That's 'cause we're forbidden from discussing it."

"By whom?"

"*Whom* do you think?" she said with a wry smile and a glance over at Margaret.

I waited.

She didn't add anything else.

"You gonna tell me?"

"Tragic accident," she said. "A very—"

"What's with all the whispering, you two?" Margaret said from behind the bar.

Susan popped up, grabbed her tray, and got back to work.

"I wasn't sayin' stop," Margaret said. "I just want in on it."

Chapter Twenty-one

On my way home, I stopped in Peachtree Pizza to pick up the pie I had ordered from Scarlett's fifteen minutes before.

It was ready and waiting—just like Rand Nola's smile.

When the customer before me left and we were alone, I said, "Got a name for you."

"Like my native name or something?" he said with an even bigger smile.

"Laney Mitchell."

His smile faded, then vanished the way Cedric and the other boys had.

"That's why you couldn't say then or now," I said.

He nodded. "How'd you . . ."

"With a little help from Susan."

"She knows?"

"She suspected."

"She's not going to say anything to Margaret, is she? It'd just upset her for no good reason."

"She's not. No one is."

"Laney loved Margaret. I mean big time. They were like the perfect couple. Lane just missed dick sometimes. That's all it was. Just sex."

Nothing is ever just sex, but I knew what he meant.

"So why did y'all stop when Cedric ran by?"

"*We* didn't. *She* did. Frustrated the hell out of me, man. She was good. I mean real good."

He looked away and was lost in reverie for a moment.

I waited for him to experience the sweetness of his memory.

"So why did she stop?" I said.

"She ran after him. Could tell he was upset. Knew something was wrong. She was such a decent person. Just took off after him. Left me there with my dick hanging out."

"What did she say?"

"Nothin'. Just took off."

"No," I said. "Later. Did she find him?"

"We never spoke again. I was still pouting when she died."

"How'd she die?"

"Dude, it was like so fuckin' sad. She was such a Good Samaritan. On her way home one night—from the bar I think—she stopped to help someone who was broken down. She was helpin' push the car the rest of the way onto the shoulder or something. Got hit by another car passing by. Hit-and-run, but they weren't sure if the driver even knew he had hit her. It was dark and raining. Who knows? Just heartbreakin' man. You know?"

I shook my head and thought about the obvious question.

"What is it?" he asked.

"Do you think it had anything to do with what happened to Cedric?"

"I never have thought about it," he said.

Maybe not such an obvious question after all.

"He's running—maybe for his life. She chases him. He disappears. She's killed soon thereafter."

"*Fuck*," he said.

"Exactly."

I had two walls now—one centered on the task force's list, Wayne Williams, and the original case, the other on Cedric and the boys who had vanished under similar circumstances. Jamal Jackson, Quentin Washington, Jaquez Anderson, Duke Ellis, and Vaughn Smith.

To this second wall I was now adding the suspicious death of Laney Mitchell. I had shared with Frank Morgan what I had discovered about Laney's actions the night of Cedric's disappearance and asked him to take a closer look at the hit-and-run report from the night she was killed.

I didn't yet know if they were one case or two, but separating out Cedric and the other still-missing victims meant I could focus on them while still searching for patterns and connections with the others.

I had made a commitment to rework the Wayne Williams case and I intended to keep it. I would continue to go back and forth between the two until I found a link between them.

So, as I ate the sausage and bacon pizza and drank Dr. Pepper, I looked for patterns and connections.

Which was what I was doing when I heard the knock at my door.

Chapter Twenty-two

I started not to answer it since nearly no one knew I lived here and Rick my roommate was at work, but before I was fully conscious of what I was doing, I was opening the front door.

When I saw who it was, I was glad I did.

There in light blue jeans and a purple Prince T-shirt was Summer Grantham with a bright, sweet smile on her face. Her blond hair was down and splayed out beautifully on her purple shoulders. A single, slender braid hung on the left side near her face.

Tonight her Keds were the same purple as her tee.

"Hey," she said.

"Hey."

"Hope you don't mind. I went to Scarlett's hoping to accidentally on purpose run into you, but you weren't there."

"I wasn't?"

"You were here instead. So I came here."

"I'm glad you did. Come in."

When she stepped inside, we hugged, and when we released one another, and for the rest of the night, her perfume clung to my clothes.

"Sorry to intrude. What am I interrupting?"

"Come and see," I said, leading her back to my room. "Excuse the place. Maid's day off."

When she walked into my room, she looked around and said, "When're you gonna unpack?"

"I have."

"Oh. You spartan by choice or necessity?"

"Uh huh," I said.

She smiled.

When her eyes came to rest on the Wayne Williams wall, she grew silent, stepped over to it, and studied it for a long while.

I waited, watching her, trying to read her reactions, attempting to see the information as if for the first time.

"No wonder you're here instead of the bar," she said, then after a pause, adding as if an afterthought, "No wonder you leave here for the bar."

When she turned toward me, she touched me very tenderly on the side of my face. Our eyes locked for a moment, something kind and caring passing between us.

Then the other wall caught her eye.

"Cedric?" she asked, stepping over to it.

I nodded and turned to follow her over to it.

"So much pain in this room," she said, reaching down and taking my hand.

We gazed at the wall for a while, our fingers laced, our breathing the only sound.

"So there are six similar cases including Cedric?" she said. "Six missing boys who never came home?"

"Do you sense anything?" I asked.

She nodded, but didn't say anything, just continued studying the scant information.

After a while, she stepped even closer and touched the wall, placed her hand on each report, every piece of paper and picture, gently caressing each one.

"They're the same in some ways, but not in others. They're more dissimilar than similar, but they are connected. But not in the way we think, not the most obvious ways."

I thought about it, deciding I didn't yet know enough about the cases for anything she was saying to resonate or be refuted.

She turned back to me again.

"I want to help you," she said.

"You have," I said. "You are."

"I want to help heal you."

"Okay."

"You're so closed, so guarded, but you haven't always been."

I nodded.

She kissed me.

I kissed her back.

The kiss became passionate and we stuck with it.

"I'd like to make love to you," she said, "to love and heal you with every part of me. Would you like to make love?"

"Is that a trick question?"

"I'm old enough to be your mother. Are you sure you'd like to? I'm not . . . You don't feel pressured, do you?"

"You're not. I want to."

"Have you had sex before? You're not a virgin, are you?"

She was so direct, so grown-up about all this that I felt completely comfortable.

"I have," I said. "Not a lot. Not enough. But I have."

Between the kissing and the frank talk about sex, I was completely aroused and ready to go.

"Take off your clothes and lie back on the bed," she said.

I did.

As I did I felt a pang of guilt and pictured Jordan watching me, but did my best to let it go.

She unhurriedly undressed.

Her body was both softer and paler than I had imagined, but beautiful and unexpectedly erotic.

My bed consisted of a box spring and a mattress, no frame, no headboard, nothing else. As usual, it was unmade.

Kneeling on the floor, she leaned up on my legs, and took me in her mouth.

Her hand and mouth moved in concert to create one of the best sensations I had experienced in my eighteen years on earth, and I felt as though something not just sexual but spiritual was taking place.

It wasn't long before I was having to resist climaxing, and she must have been able to tell, because she stopped what she was doing and began kissing my body, working her way up to my mouth.

It felt as if she were kissing every inch of me, the nipples of her large, low-slung breasts grazing my skin as she did. Eventually, she reached my lips and began kissing me with her warm, wet mouth.

Leaving my mouth, she kissed her way over to my ear.

There she began whispering with the voice of God.

"You are so loved, John. So loved. You are whole. Everything you need is in you already. You are adored, John. So adored. You are precious and valued and most of all loved. So very loved. Let go of everything within you blocking the love of God from flowing in you and through you. Let love in. Let pain and darkness out. Let go. Let be. Breathe love. Be love."

She then straddled me, took me in her hand, and slid me inside her.

As we began moving slowly, rhythmically, she leaned down and I took her breasts in my hands. Cupping, caressing, loving.

I then lifted my head, my mouth finding her erect nipples, and I experienced something equal parts erotic and nurturing, and for the first time in a long time I felt connected, felt alive, felt loved.

Chapter Twenty-three

I woke up from the deepest, most restful sleep I had experienced in a very long time.

The room was dark.

Beside me, still naked, Summer slept soundly, her warmth and steady breathing reassuring and buoying somehow.

I glanced at the GE clock with the green digital display on the stack of books beside my bed. It was a graduation present from a family friend and my kindergarten teacher. The Merriam-Webster's Collegiate Dictionary it sat on was a gift on the same occasion from my aunt and fourth grade teacher.

It was a little after three in the morning.

Easing out of the bed, I slipped into the bathroom, peed and washed my face.

The bedroom was cold, the bathroom colder.

Seeing my naked body in the mirror, knowing there was a naked woman I had made love to earlier in my warm bed, made me feel more mature, more like an adult, than anything in my life leading up to this moment, and I liked the way it felt.

When I opened the door to walk back into the bedroom, a shaft of light fell across the Cedric Porter wall, illuminating what I had been about to study when Summer first knocked on my door.

Leaving the door ajar, I stepped over to the wall and began to read the information on it.

After a while, I walked over to the two bookshelves and the small table I used for a desk in the corner opposite my bed. Feeling around in the semi-dark, I located pen and paper, then returned to the wall.

Following Chet Dettlinger's lead, I made a map of the six victims on the wall. Because they had never been found, I could only mark the spots where they had lived and last been seen.

It didn't take long to perceive the pattern.

Like the Atlanta Child Murder victims of Dettlinger's map, at least five of the six on my map had a connection to Memorial Drive.

Though it was the same Memorial Drive, it might as well not have been. It was the opposite end, as different as the intercity and the suburbs. The victims on Dettlinger's map were inside the perimeter, downtown, on the mean streets of Moreland and MLK. The victims on my map were connected to the strip of Memorial outside the perimeter, between I-285 and Stone Mountain.

The different worlds of the two sets of victims were worlds apart, and didn't seem to be connected. There were plenty of connections within each group, but the two groups didn't seem to be connected to each other in any way—at least not in any way I had discovered yet.

"Bring that cute ass back to bed," Summer said.

I turned to see her looking up at me in a sleepy, sexy way that made me want to do just that.

"Just a few more minutes," I said.

"You can turn on the light."

"It's okay. Sorry I woke you."

"You found something, didn't you?" she said.

"Think so."

"Tell me."

I climbed back in bed, switched on the small lamp on the stack of books beside the clock, and showed her my map.

"This is Memorial Drive," I said, pointing to my inept sketch. "This is where we are, where Cedric lived. This is where he disappeared from. All these little houses are where the other boys lived. The stick figures are where they went missing from."

She yawned, rubbed her eyes, and studied the map. "They're all right around here," she said.

"All but one."

"One actually lived in this same apartment complex?" she said.

I nodded. "Jamal Jackson. He and Cedric played together some."

"Oh my God."

"These two, Quentin Washington and Jaquez Anderson, lived in an apartment complex on the other side of Memorial less than a block down. Duke Ellis lived in a house down off North Hairston. The only one who doesn't fit is Vaughn Smith. He lived over off Wesley Chapel."

"You think maybe he shouldn't be in this group?" she asked.

"I don't know."

"I feel like he should," she said. "I can't explain it, but . . ."

"Then he probably does," I said. "We'll keep searching until we find a connection."

"Speaking of connection," she said. "How would you like to connect again before we go back to sleep?"

Chapter Twenty-four

The next morning, I attended classes with a smile on my face.

I felt more alive and alert and awake than I had in quite a while—and it showed. Several people, including LaDonna Paulk and Randy Renfroe, commented on it.

After classes and a quick lunch, I whistled my way through my janitorial work at the college, cleaning the classrooms and bathrooms with extra vigor. As I did, my thoughts alternated between my experience with Summer and what I had uncovered on the cases so far.

My limited sexual experience had not prepared me for my encounter with Summer. Prior to her there had only been two girls my age, both of whom were as inexperienced and inept as I was—and they both expected me to take the lead. With Summer, a mature, experienced woman, I was dealing with a skilled, generous lover who not only healed but taught, who not only led, but taught me how to.

The classroom door opened and I turned.

"Someone here to see you," Randy said. "A police officer. Is everything okay?"

I shrugged. "I have no idea."

I began walking toward the staircase with him.

"Where were you just then?" he asked.

"Huh?"

"You were a million miles away with the textbook definition of contentment on your face."

"Was I?"

"You were. It's good to see."

"I'm having so many incredible experiences," I said. "Learning so much. I'm so glad I came up here."

We reached the stairs and began walking up them.

"You are?" he said.

"I am."

"You haven't seemed so for a while," he said. "I thought with what happened with Safe Haven and all you were . . ."

"I was. But then I . . . met someone . . . and had an entirely new experience of God."

"Well," he said, a big, amused smile on his face. "How about that?"

Upstairs, Randy returned to his office and I walked out the main entrance to find Bobby Battle and another detective I didn't recognize waiting on me.

Both men wore their shield on the left front side of their belt, their holstered .45 on their right. Both wore a suit, though Battle's was much more stylish than the other man's.

"John Jordan, Detective Remy Boss."

We shook hands.

"We were close by and decided to stop in and try to talk some sense into you before you do something stupid," Battle said.

"You arrived just in the nick of time," I said.

"Did I mention he's a smart-ass?" Battle said to Boss.

"Seemed an appropriate response to me," he said.

I smiled.

"So what can I tell you?" Remy said.

"You investigated the disappearances of Cedric Porter, Jamal Jackson, Quentin Washington, Jaquez Anderson, Duke Ellis, and Vaughn Smith?"

"No, just Porter, Jackson, and Anderson, but I'm familiar with all of them."

"I'd appreciate it if you'd tell me anything you recall about the cases," I said.

"Sure, and by the way, I thought Larry Moore was a wife-beating asshole. Fuck brothers in blue when a man hits a woman."

I nodded.

"Okay, the cases. Most of 'em happened during the missing and murdered kids case so we took them very seriously, conducted righteous investigations. All single moms, all streetwise, latchkey kids raising themselves, all better off with their dads or whichever family member decided to give them a real home."

"How certain are you that's what happened?" I asked.

"Fairly," he said. "I mean, between you and me, I would've liked to be more so, but as I said it was the height of the serial killings and we were stretched pretty damn thin."

He seemed to have more to say so I waited.

"You gotta remember how it was back then. In those days, you didn't find a body, you knew the kid was alive, more than likely okay somewhere, you had to move on. Our theory was that the dads saw what was happening with the murders, how similar their kids were to the kids being killed, and decided to remove them from the very situations that made them targets. We weren't about to take the kids and put them back in the most dangerous possible position they could be in."

"Did you ever see the boys with their dads?"

"We would have, but we didn't have that kind of time. It would've taken tailing the dads, staking out their pads. Best we could do was find evidence they had them."

"Such as?"

"Toys, games, clothes, their schedules altered around school, change in routine. In Jamal's case we found the outfit he was last seen in among his clothes and things at his dad's. In most cases the dads told us it was stuff their kids kept there from when they visited, though I'm not sure they really knew, but Jamal's dad having the clothes he was last seen wearing proved it wasn't just that."

I thought about it. Some of what he said made sense, but there were lots of holes in it too. I knew how bad things were back then, how a dead body turning up trumped a missing kid every time, but it didn't make it right or justify sloppy, lazy, or incomplete police work.

"Only exception was Cedric's dad," he said. "He was the least helpful in our investigation, and we didn't turn up anything of Cedric's at his place, in his car, nowhere."

"Okay?" Battle said. "That enough for you? Can we go back to fighting real crime now?"

That afternoon, I drove out to Ellenwood, to Fairview Memorial Gardens, to Jordan's plot near the stone statue of Saint Mark.

It was a bright, clear day. I preferred the times it was raining when I visited.

"Last time I was here I said I wasn't coming back," I

said.

Next to me, Saint Mark remained implacable, silent witness to my quandary and misery.

"I thought I meant it, but . . . I'm having such a hard time letting go—of you, of what happened. I'm angry and embarrassed and . . . I just can't . . . I haven't been able to get over it all . . . over you . . . yet. And on top of everything else . . . that really bothers me. I should've been able to let go a long time ago, to . . . I don't know."

I looked over at the bearded and robed apostle holding his tablet.

"You ever seen anything like this? You're not taking notes, are you?"

Like Jordan, he didn't respond.

"Ever experience anything like this?" I asked him. "Ever have that stone heart of yours broken?"

Still nothing.

I looked back at Jordan's headstone.

"Eventually, I will stop doing this," I said. "I'll get better. I'll heal. I'll get over you. Just not today."

Chapter Twenty-five

Annie Mae Dozier was a small, gray-haired black woman with thick glasses above freckled cheeks. She wore a simple cotton sheath dress over her thin, narrow frame, and sank so far into the worn sheet-covered couch, a good portion of her wasn't visible. Like everything else in the place, the blue and white dress was old and faded and looked like something from the sixties to me.

Her apartment was even more modestly furnished than mine.

"He was such a good boy," she said, blinking behind her big glasses. "Smart. Sweet. He was my little buddy."

"He came over here a lot?" I asked.

She nodded her shrunken head. "Fair amount, that's a fact. Every time his no-good mama go down to the bar or have mens over . . . I'd hear a little tapatap on my door. He say, 'Aunt Annie, you got any of them little cookies like I likes?' I always did. I'd feed him, let him watch a video—he always had a video and his uncle gave me a VCR so he could watch 'em over here. He do that or color or both. He loved movies and loved to color. And he loved his Aunt Annie. And I loved him. He the closest thing to a grandchild I'a ever have. Only got one daughter and she ain't able to have no youngins."

"Did he ever confide in you?" I asked.

"Certainly. He get upset, this the first place he come. I talk to him. Rub his back. Directly he calm down and be back to his happy little self."

"What kinds of things upset him?" I asked.

"Ima notta gonna lie. His whole life was upsetting. Yes sir, it was."

"Was he worried about anything? Scared of anything? Anybody bothering him leading up to his disappearance?"

"He always worried 'bout somethin'. Mama like that . . . he never know she gonna hug him or hit him. Never know when he gonna eat again. No food in the house. Never know when them mens she have over gonna try to mess with him."

"Sexually, you mean?"

She frowned and nodded. "Some came just for him. No interest in that old drunk. She pass out and they mess with little Cedric. I call the police, but they ain't do nothin' 'bout it. Then on, she have a man over, Cedric stay over here. I fix him up his own little room—well a corner of my daughter's room. She was finishin' up her schoolin'. Hardly ever here. Didn't mind at all, no sir. She like Cedric. Everybody did. She done grown up and moved out now. She a pharmacist down to McDonough. So proud of that girl. Directly, I be movin' down there with her. Help out. She make good money, that's a fact."

"Did he mention anyone messing with him or anything he was worried about in the weeks leading up to his disappearance?" I asked.

It was the same question phrased in a slightly different way. She hadn't really answered it the first time.

"No, sir. No more than usual. Nothin' that stands

out."

I started to say something, but her tired, old eyes opened wide and she held her bony-fingered hand up.

"Wait just a minute there now," she said. "Almost forgots about . . . Creepy bothered with him a bit more than usual 'round that time, I do believe."

"Creepy?"

"That what the kids called him," she said. "Real name was Daryl Lee Gibbons or Gibsons. Somethin' like that. Creepy fit him, yes sir it most certainly did that. He wasn't quite right in the head, eyes crossed, always staring after the kids. Big, fat, slow-movin' white boy. Always creepin' up on you. One minute he just there. In the shadows, gazing, licking his lips."

"What did he do to Cedric?"

"Nothin' far as I know, just followed him around like the rest of the kids, starin', gruntin', talkin' gibberish. But I seem to recall him bein' 'round more 'round that time. Cedric mentionin' him followin' him even more."

"Where does he live?"

"Creepy? Moved right after Cedric disappeared. Good riddance. No idea where he be at now. Just not here, thank God."

"What do you think happened to Cedric?" I asked.

She shrugged. "Somebody snatch him. Grab him up, take him away, do things to him, kill him and bury him in some woods somewhere. That what was happenin' back then. Boys just like him—no one lookin' out for 'em. Snatched. Strangled. Dumped. Gone. Forever."

"Do you remember a guy who used to live in Memorial Manor the kids called Creepy?" I asked.

I had stopped by Second Chances after leaving

Annie Mae's and on my way to return my movies to
Lonnie's.

"Not just the kids," Camille Pollard said. "We all
called Daryl Lee Gibbons that."

She was just as stylishly dressed and looked just as
tired as when Mickey had introduced me to her.

"Do you think he could've taken Cedric or the other
kids?"

She shrugged. "I guess it crossed my mind, but . . .
Daryl Lee just seemed too slow—mentally and physically,
too simple. Seemed to me more like he wanted to be a kid,
or thought he was, than wanted to hurt one. Either way, I
always kept my kids away from him. They were younger,
of course, but . . . The thing is . . . I've always thought the
killer—or killers, if there are two—are black. And not just
'cause they'd have a better chance of going unnoticed, but
because . . . You familiar with the concept of self-hatred?"

I nodded, finding it a bit difficult to take her
seriously with her asymmetrical bob bobbing about.

"For some people it runs very deep. Minorities, the
poor, the marginalized and disenfranchised are culturally
conditioned by the majority, the power structure, to hate
themselves. It's so entrenched, so deeply ingrained most
don't even know they do it."

She spoke with conviction, but it sounded like
something she had heard or had read—perhaps in a
college class or special lecture on race and culture she had
attended.

"But you can't be oppressed and tortured and told
that it's your fault and you're worthless and it not have
an effect on you," she continued. "You can't be poor and
without possibilities when everyone else has plenty, and
plenty more coming—all while they're telling you the
reason you don't have more and don't do better is because

you're slow and stupid and lazy and ignorant and criminal and—without it causing you to start to believe it yourself. Think about a kid in a family being told that he's less than. He grows up believing it. If he's also told that or made to feel that way by a teacher, he believes it even more. But what if everywhere you look, everything you hear, every single thread sewn into the fabric of your life, of life itself, was telling you that you and your family and your kin and kind are inferior, less than—not just a nigger, but a nigger for a reason. Women are told it. Jews are told it. So many are told it. But no one is told it like black people in America. I've always thought the killer was a self-hating black person."

I thought about it—about how this black woman who was dating a white man and had straightened her hair and dressed and spoke in a way many would describe as white, was speaking so eloquently of self-hating black people.

"But," she added, "we did mention Creepy to the police back then—both when Jamal and Cedric went missing. Don't know what they did about it. Then he vanished too. One day he was here. The next he was gone. Nobody knew where he went."

"Okay, thanks," I said.

"Let me tell you a dirty little secret," she said.

"What's that?"

As usual, her shop was empty, but she still lowered her voice.

"All the kids who got snatched back then . . . all those poor missing and murdered children . . . went missing and got murdered 'cause nobody was watching them like they should."

Blame the victim, I thought. *It's what Job's so-called friends did. It's what far too many people do. Who's practicing self-hating now?*

"I'm not sayin' they should've been taken or killed, just that if they were where they were supposed to be and being watched like they should've been, it wouldn't've happened."

I remember hearing Wayne Williams say something just like that.

"But Cedric's is a special case. His mom's the worst. Sorry as the day is long. So what if she had a rough childhood. So what if she been abused or mistreated or . . . whatever. It's no excuse. It's no reason to . . . be like she was with her boy. She's as self-hating as anyone I've ever seen—and not without reason. Wouldn't be at all surprised if she didn't kill her own boy."

"**W**hat can you tell me about Daryl Lee Gibbons?" I said.

Lonnie frowned, shook his head, and looked down.

I waited.

"How'd you find out?" he said.

"Find out what?"

"What I did. That's not why you're asking?"

"His name came up. Just trying to find out what I can about him."

"He didn't take Cedric," he said.

"How do you know that?"

"Because . . . I thought he did."

I waited, but he didn't say anything else.

"I don't understand," I said.

"I beat that boy bad. Real bad. Back when Cedric went missing. Creepy was the first place I went. Searched his apartment. Questioned him. I was convinced he had taken Cedric. I was out of my mind with . . . I was real messed up. Convinced Creepy had hurt and killed him and buried him in the woods between here and the apartment complex. I beat him so bad I believed he'd've told me if he had done anything to my boy."

I nodded.

"I'm ashamed of what I did, but I can't say I wouldn't do it again."

"I understand."

We were quiet a moment.

"Did he report you?" I asked.

He shook his head. "Have no idea why."

"Guilty people avoid the cops," I said.

"You think he . . . and I . . . let him go?"

I shrugged. "Not saying that. Just that it might be a possibility. Or that he was guilty of something else."

"Or that his life was such shit he just expected treatment like that," he said.

I remembered the movies in my hand and set them on the counter.

"Keep 'em. I know you ain't watched 'em yet."

"You sure?"

He nodded.

"Thanks."

"Be good to see you back at a meeting," he said.

"I will be soon," I said. "Soon as I can. It helped. I'm doin' better. I'll be back. Count on it."

"I will, then."

"I hear Daryl Lee just disappeared," I said. "Here one day. Gone the next. Do you know why or where he went?"

He shook his head. "No idea. Hope it wasn't 'cause of what I did to him or, even more so, because of something he did and I let him go, but . . . it was around that same time."

"Sorry to have to ask this," I began, then paused.

"What?"

"Your sister."

He shook his head. "Don't hold back. Finding Cedric is all that matters—and I know how she . . . what a mess she is."

"I think she's lying," I said.

"She definitely is," he said. "It just has nothing to do with Cedric's disappearance—least not that I could ever find. She's lying about where she was and when she finally made it to the bar because she was scoring some dope or turnin' a trick. Probably is indirectly why Cedric got snatched—'cause she wasn't tendin' to him—but I never found anything to say she was directly involved. And believe me I looked. And if I had, I wouldn't cover it up. She had her chance to grow up and become something, to change and be better, and she didn't. Cedric didn't get his."

"You got yours and you took it," I said. "And AA is a big part of it, isn't it?"

"The biggest. Ada is lost. Nothin' I can do about that. But Cedric . . . I was gonna make sure he made it out, made something of himself. I was gonna . . . He was gonna have a good life."

Chapter Twenty-six

Mickey Davis and I were at the Varsity to see Cedric Porter, Sr.

It was late, and the world's largest drive-in was mostly empty, its large rooms vacant, its tables in need of bussing.

We had arrived a little earlier than planned, and it would be another half hour or so until Cedric Sr. finished his shift. And though we hadn't come to eat, since we were here with a little extra time on our hands we agreed we'd be fools not to.

"What'll you have?" the large African-American woman behind the counter asked.

She wore a red shirt, white apron, a red Varsity paper hat, and the weariness of a woman needing a break from her life.

I had a cheeseburger, fries, a fried apple pie, and a Coke. Mickey had a couple of chili cheese dogs, onion rings, and a Frosted Orange.

While we waited, I read a few statistics about this unique place from a plaque on the wall. It's the world's largest single outlet for Coke. It can hold six hundred cars and eight hundred people. Every single day it serves more than two miles of hotdogs, one ton of onion rings, five thousand fried pies, and twenty-five hundred pounds of potatoes. On Georgia Tech game days some thirty thousand people come here to eat.

I thought about Rudy's little roadside diner in Pottersville and said aloud, "We're not in Kansas anymore."

"No we're not," Mickey said.

We carried our red trays of food up some stairs and into one of the empty rooms, and ate the way men do when women aren't around.

That thought made me miss Summer and long to be with her in my bed again soon.

"Guess who's got a record?" Mickey asked, his soft voice hard to hear in the empty, open space of the room.

"Who's that?"

"Creepy Gibbons. Took less than ten minutes and two calls to turn up."

I hadn't mentioned Daryl Lee to him. Camille must have.

"For what?" I asked.

"A little L and L."

He had started making a little more eye contact with me, but only a little. He still mostly had the eyes of a shy and insecure child.

Lewd and lascivious acts are any touches to the genitals, breasts, or butt of a minor—clothed or not.

"No details yet," he said. "Have no idea what he did, where, or when, but should know tomorrow."

What if he was responsible for what happened to Cedric and the others? What if that's why he moved right after? What if the murders didn't stop, just changed locations? What if he was missed somehow in the original investigation?

Eventually, Cedric Porter, Sr. joined us.

He was still wearing his red paper hat and white apron. The apron was soiled with grease and smeared with ketchup—which looked like dirt and bloodstains.

Beneath his paper hat, he was bald, his large head smooth and gleaming. Below it, the rest of his body was big and round like his head.

"Tired and ready to go home," he said as he collapsed into the booth with us. "What this about?"

"Cedric, Jr.," I said.

"What about him?" he asked, defensive. "Whatta two white boys got to do with a missin' black boy?"

"We're tryin' to find him," I said. "Reinvestigating his case along with some other similar ones."

"Coulda save you a trip," he said. "Never had nothin' to do with that boy. Didn't take 'im. Don't have 'im. Don't know nothin' about who did."

Not quite sure what to say to that, we were all quiet a moment.

I glanced over at Mickey. He shrugged. He had yet to offer anything to the conversation. Why start now?

"Look," Cedric said. "His mama crazy. Okay? She gave that kid my name 'cause she wanted to give him a name other than her own. He wasn't my kid. I got kids. I take care of 'em. Why I work this lame-ass job. Why I'm too tired to talk about this shit. I didn't have nothin' to do with him 'cause he wasn't mine and his mama a crazy-ass bitch tryin' to run a con on me. That's it. That's all I know."

He began pushing his enormous girth up out of the booth, the table and bench creaking from the strain.

"One more question," I said.

"If it quick," he said, standing over us now.

"Do you have any idea who his actual father was?"

"No. Not really. Lots of candidates. Why?"

"Because," I said, "maybe that's who took him."

Chapter Twenty-seven

All day I had hoped to hear from Summer.

Since I had no way of getting in touch with her, no idea where she lived or what her number was, my only option was to wait and hope to hear from her.

I had come straight back to my apartment after leaving the Varsity, hoping she'd be here waiting for me.

She was not.

I hung around for a while, trying to do homework and work on the cases while waiting for her to call.

She did not.

After a while I gave up and walked to Scarlett's.

The dark path was spooky and seemed dangerous, and I wondered if Cedric was buried somewhere in these woods.

I heard something a few feet off the path and turned.

Through the bushes I could see a middle-aged white man leaning against a tree, his trousers down around his knees, a young black woman kneeling in front performing fellatio on him.

Were Ronald Nolan and Laney Mitchell doing something similar when little Cedric ran by? Is that the way it really happened? Why was Cedric headed back to the apartments? Had he forgotten something? Did he see something or someone who scared him? Was Nolan telling the truth?

Make mine a double and keep 'em coming," I said to Margaret as I reached the end of the bar and the stool I thought of as mine.

"I'll join you," she said. "It's been a day."

"Wait," Susan said, walking up behind me. "You've been doin' so well."

"I'm still doin' well," I said, climbing onto the barstool.

"Then don't blow it by jumpin' down this particular rabbit hole. There's nothin' good at the bottom of it. You've got to know that better than me."

I looked at Margaret.

"I could just as easily pour you coffee," she said.

"Et tu?"

She shrugged. "Let's both have coffee tonight."

"I'll talk about the case with you," Susan said. "You can ask me anything you want. And when I get off in a little while I'll even go back to your place and watch a movie with you. Whatta you have?"

"*Sixteen Candles*—"

"My favorite."

"*Oh sexy girlfriend,*" Margaret said in her best Asian accent.

"Lots of sugar," I said.

They both voiced their approval.

Margaret poured the coffee and shoved cream and sugar toward me as Susan climbed up on the stool beside me.

I had not mentioned Laney Mitchell to either of them again. As far as I knew neither of them had any idea she had run after Cedric the night he disappeared or that doing so might be connected to what happened to her. And they weren't going to hear it from me—not until I found out if there was anything to it. So I decided to pursue another line of questioning with them instead.

"What do y'all know about Creepy Daryl Lee Gibbons?" I said.

"He scared Cedric," Susan said.

"I know Lonnie beat the shit out of him tryin' to find Cedric," Margaret said. "Don't blame him. He was the most likely suspect we had. If there was even a chance he had taken Cedric, that he could still be alive, he had to try to find out . . . no matter what it took."

"What it took was twenty-three stitches and a lot of bandages and pain meds," Susan said.

"I don't think Creepy was the only one Lonnie pummeled tryin' to find out what happened," Margaret added.

"You don't remember him being around here that night, do you?" I said. "Could he be who Cedric was running from?"

"Didn't see him. Don't think he was around. Can't tell you how many times I've wondered and worried if it was someone coming in or going out of here that night that killed him."

A thought occurred to me—one I couldn't believe I hadn't had before—one I had to act on immediately.

"Can I borrow your phone?" I asked.

"Sure," Margaret said, "but be a lot quieter to use the payphone outside. Here's a quarter."

"Thanks."

It was late, but this couldn't wait. I was sure I would

wake him—him and his sweet wife, but I couldn't not call him right now.

The phone booth was at the end of the lot down near the sidewalk on Memorial Drive.

I walked directly to it, stone cold sober, light but steady traffic streaking by on Memorial.

Dropping the quarter in, I dialed the number I had long since memorized.

Frank Morgan answered trying not to sound like I had just woken him up.

"I want to meet with him," I said.

"John?"

"Sorry, yeah."

"You okay?"

"I am."

"You sure?"

"I want to meet with him, Frank."

"Who?"

"You know who. Can you set it up?"

"It'll take some doin', and I'll have to be there, but yeah, if you can pass a background check, I can set it up."

"Would you?"

"I will."

"Thank you," I said. "Not sure if I've told you lately, but you've been a grace to me—one of the few since I've been here. And 'less you think that's drink talking, I haven't had one in awhile."

I started to hang up.

"Before you go," he said. "I spoke with the attorney representing Martin Fisher's mother. Told him how good you were to the kid, how bad the mom was, how you took care of him and never even saw her the entire time they were your neighbors. Told him to reconsider."

"What'd he say?"

"That if he didn't take the case someone else would. I told him we'd produce credible witnesses to refute everything the absentee mother said and that supported everything you said—including law enforcement officers."

"What'd he say to that?"

"Says that's the way it works. We produce witnesses and they produce witnesses. Wouldn't back down. I told him the only thing of value you owned was a VCR—and that it wasn't worth that much. And that's when he let it slip."

"What?"

"Since you were living in what was technically a college dorm, he thinks they can get EPI and Chapel Hill Harvester Church to settle for a sizable chunk of change."

"Oh my God," I said.

The blow was devastating—the embarrassment alone was more than I could handle, but to have the church and college on the line for something I was involved in?

"It's the way people like this think."

"I . . . I can't . . . I don't know what to say. It's too much."

"Don't get ahead of yourself. I haven't given up on this. We'll get it straightened out."

After hanging up, I was too upset to go back into Scarlett's right away.

For a while I just paced around the mostly empty parking lot.

"You okay?"

I turned to see Lonnie locking the front door of his video store.

I shrugged.

"What is it?"

I told him. Not in detail but enough to give him a

sense of what I was dealing with.

"You know what to do," he said. "Don't need me to tell you. Let go of what you can't change anyway and change what you can. Breathe in peace. Breathe out worry and stress. You can do it. Say the Serenity Prayer with me."

I did.

"Again."

This time he took my hand in his as we prayed the prayer together again.

"God grant me the serenity to accept thing things I cannot change, the courage to change the things I can, and the wisdom to know the difference."

"Thank you," I said.

"You gonna be okay? I can call the guys over and we can have a meeting right now."

"I'm okay. Thanks."

"Not thinking about drinking, are you?"

I shook my head.

"Will you call me if you need anything?" he asked. "Anything at all?"

"I will. And thanks again."

Chapter Twenty-eight

Though Susan had offered to come back and watch a movie with me, I went home alone.

I was upset by the news Frank had given me, but I was also hoping Summer would come over at some point.

Perhaps. But that was only part of it. I wanted to work my walls, compile the information I had received so far, to look over things in the light of the new details I now had.

I intended to go straight in and get to work.

What I did instead was collapse onto my bed and fall fast asleep.

Soon I was dreaming.

Summer and I were standing in the woods between Memorial Manor and Scarlett's, talking about Cedric and the other still-missing boys when they began to rise out of the ground around us.

Digging, scratching, scooping, they clawed their way out of their shallow graves, their faces, hair, and clothes caked with dirt and mud, twigs and bugs sticking to their hair, dried blood clinging to their soiled and tattered clothes.

I was saying something when I woke up but had no idea what.

When I went back to sleep, Mickey Davis was demonstrating how easy it would be to snatch a kid. One moment we were riding in his car on I-20 toward downtown, the next he was pulling up to a street corner where a barefooted, shirtless young black boy in only cutoffs was walking home with a can of snuff.

"Get in," Mickey said.

The kid did as he was told.

"See?" he said to me.

"Yeah, see?" the kid said. "Nothing to it."

"What does it mean?" I asked.

"Nothing," they said in unison. "Nothing means nothing."

The next morning, during a discussion in my New Testament class, I was struck by how different I was from the other students, how different my experience was from theirs.

It wasn't just that their paradigm and approach to religion and the Bible was far more concrete and literal than mine, it was that this classroom, the school, the church, the practice of their faith was all consuming. I was sure they must, but it didn't seem like they had a life outside of the school and the church.

Maybe it wasn't that they didn't have one, but the way being part of the school and being a member of the church defined, dictated, and determined their lives entire.

There had been a special service at the church the night before. I was the only one not in attendance.

When I offered a dissenting opinion, a different way of seeing the same dynamic—namely God's work in the world—I was told that I just didn't get it. I would have if

I had attended the service, heard the bishop's message, a message they referred to as the rest of the revelation.

"God's only work in the world is through his church," one student said. "It's only those aligned with his purpose, his set-aside and chosen people, who can come into agreement with him to bring about his kingdom on this planet."

It must have been obvious that I didn't agree.

"You disagree?" he said to me.

"I do."

When I didn't elaborate, he said, "Why?"

"Your supposition is rooted in tribalism," I said. "It's the old us-and-them formulation. I don't see it that way. I think grace flows through whoever allows it to. To label a group of people as special, as the only ones used by God isn't just imperceptive, it's dangerous. It's the same kind of thinking that says there's no truth outside of a particular sacred text, or a specific spokesperson for God. It's limiting to the point of absurdity. If there's a God, a creative, loving force that transcends being itself, she can't be limited to a single religion, book, prophet, or—"

"Pronoun, evidently," another student said.

"Exactly. It's like Paul Tillich said—'God isn't a being, but the ground of all being.'"

"Tillich also said 'the first duty of love is to listen,'" Dan Rhodes, the professor, said. "We need to make sure we're all doing that, all listening to one another."

What if Martin's mother's lawsuit causes all this to go away? What if it damages it beyond repair? What if I'm responsible for that?

It felt funny to keep calling her *Martin's mother*, but I had never met the woman, didn't know anything about her—including her name.

I nodded. "Sorry if I didn't listen like I should."

"I'm not saying you didn't," he said. "Just reminding us all that we need to. Let's listen to John some more. Share with us what you're feeling, what you're hearing, what you'd like to say."

"Thank you. I don't have answers, only questions. I believe the religious experience can be approached as a way of having all the answers or as a way of having none, of only having profound questioning. Back to Tillich—this will be the last time I quote him today, I promise. He said something to the effect that being religious means asking passionately the question of the meaning of our existence and being willing to receive answers, even when they hurt. For me . . . I just feel . . . like maybe our conversations and explorations are sometimes too confining, too reductive for the topics we're discussing. I'm sure it's just me, though. Thanks for letting me share that."

He nodded. "You make a good point. We believe we've been created in the image of God. We must be careful not to return the favor."

"I don't understand," another student said.

"We have to make sure we're not making God over into our image, that we're not making an idol out of ourselves—our own beliefs and preferences and limitations and superstitions."

"Which I know I'm guilty of," I said.

"We all are. First step is to recognize it. Can't deal with it until we do."

That made me think of AA and Lonnie's small, sincere group, and I committed to going later in the day.

Thinking of Lonnie led me to Cedric and gave me an idea. It would require yet another favor from Frank Morgan—something I had to be getting close to exhausting but had yet to.

Thinking of Frank in the context of this class and

conversation made me think of how much good he did in the world, how much the force of God worked through him, though he would never see it that way. He was not a member of any church, wasn't religious in any way but the ways that mattered.

"Sorry again for waking you up last night," I said.

"No problem," he said.

I was in Randy Renfroe's office after class, calling Saint Frank.

"Not so sorry to keep me from asking for another favor or two, though."

He laughed.

"It's just a thought I had," I said. "Remember me tellin' you that Ada Baker claims her son Cedric calls her from time to time?"

"Yeah?"

"Could we put a trace on her phone so we can track down whoever it is doing the calling—if there is someone?"

"It's a great idea," he said. "I just don't know logistically if it's something I can get done. What's the other?"

"Trying to find a guy named Daryl Lee Gibbons."

"What's his story?" he asked.

I told him.

"Tell you what," he said. "You commit to going home for the holidays and really make an effort to patch things up with your dad, and I'll see what I can do about both. Deal?"

I thought about it for a moment. Thanksgiving was a few weeks away, and I had pretty much decided to stay up here that weekend, but . . .

"Deal," I said. "Thanks, Frank."

"Oh, I almost forgot. That hit-and-run you asked about."

"Yeah?"

"No evidence that it was anything but," he said. "In fact, cop on the scene theorized that maybe the driver didn't even know he'd done it. There were no skid marks. Looks like he never even braked."

"Which is exactly how it would look if it wasn't an accident."

When I ended my call with Frank, I walked across the hall to the chapel.

Classes completed, students gone for the day, most of the small staff at lunch, the chapel was empty, quiet, and dark, just the way I liked it.

For a while I just walked around the chapel, thinking, praying, wrestling with my mind.

I was missing Summer, agitated that I hadn't heard from her. I was anxious about the cases, the lawsuit, my conflict with my fellow students and my estrangement from my dad, and many other things I needed to let go of.

Which was what I was here for.

"God grant me the serenity to accept the things I cannot change," I said aloud into the silence of the sacred space, "the courage the change the things I can, and the wisdom to know the difference."

After a while of saying it, I began to practice it, and eventually I began to feel somewhat centered again.

Chapter Twenty-nine

That afternoon I went to the AA meeting in Lonnie's storage room.

I was sitting across from a partially visible poster of *Dressed to Kill*, the Brian De Palma Hitchcockian erotic thriller with Michael Caine and Angie Dickinson. The top of the poster read "Brian De Palma, the master of the macabre, invites you to a special showing of the latest fashion . . . in murder."

It peeked out from behind a shelf of cat food and cases of Coke—the latter Lonnie both sold and consumed.

As we said the Serenity Prayer and went over the Twelve Steps, I realized I had been using them to deal with Summer's disappearance from my life, the lawsuit, the case. Rather than remaining upset or so out of sorts I wasn't good for much of anything else, I had practiced accepting what I couldn't change and changed what I could.

The process and practice of AA didn't just work for alcohol addiction.

"I want to talk about something today that we can all fall victim to," Lonnie said. "Being dry drunks—something that happens when we stop drinking but don't change our mentalities, don't change our stinking thinking."

The two other men nodded as if they knew what he

was talking about.

"Sobriety isn't just stopping the consumption of alcohol," he said. "It's a way of life, of being. It's a complete change in our way of thinking, behaving, living. It can only happen when we deal with our defects of character."

"Drinking is a symptom not the disease," one of the other men added.

"Exactly."

"Drinking is our way of dealing with the disease," the other man said. "The worst way."

Lonnie nodded. "We have to be so careful," he said. "We can so easily fool ourselves. We can replace drink with another obsession and think we're sober when we're not, when we haven't changed a thing."

That's when I realized all this was for my benefit. He had saved this particular discussion for when I was present.

He thought I had traded alcohol for the investigation into his nephew's disappearance and that of the Atlanta Child Murders. And he was right.

I was a dry drunk and needed to hear what he had to say, but that didn't mean I wanted or was going to.

Later that afternoon, Mickey and I located Jamal Jackson's biological father and began following him.

Our plan was to follow all the fathers to see if any of them had their sons as the cops had theorized. Of course, some of the kids would be my age by now, and could be out on their own. If they were between ten and fourteen when they were taken, they would be between fifteen and nineteen now.

We started with Jamal's father because we had to

start somewhere and he was the first we found.

The first afternoon, we followed him together. From then on we alternated, changing out when we could, covering as much of the day as we could while still meeting our other obligations. Mickey had more flexible time than I did and took more shifts.

Gerry Jackson, Jamal's father, worked at night as a cook at the Waffle House on Panola Road. When he was at work, we mostly watched his house. When he wasn't, we mostly watched him, searching for any sign of Jamal.

After three days, two of which were on a weekend, we had found no sign of Jamal.

On the fourth day, we showed up at Gerry's place of work, took a booth and ordered breakfast like any other customers.

It was the middle of the night, and the place was mostly empty. When Gerry finished his final order and had a break, we asked if we could talk to him.

"Somethin' wrong with your food?" he asked.

"No, it's perfect," I said. "Very good. Please, sit down with us for just a minute."

He slowly, warily sat down, studying us as he did. "What's this about?"

"Jamal," I said.

"Y'all have him?" he said, sitting up, ready to fight.

"Nothing like that," I said. "We're looking for him."

"Whatcha mean?"

"We're part of a group looking for missing children," I said. "He's a reporter. I'm a student. We're all volunteers trying to do something the police didn't or couldn't."

"Man, don't get me started on the fuckin' cops," he said. "Didn't do shit but blame me. Convinced my ex I took Jamal from her. She still think I did. She stalk me. Sue me. Say all kind of shit about me, but I didn't take my boy.

Could have if I wanted to. After all, he's my son, just as much as hers. But I didn't."

"Any idea who might have?" I asked.

As usual, Mickey wasn't saying much, just taking notes and taking it all in. He had told me this was his preferred way to work. By letting me ask the questions, he could focus on the person we were talking to and his writing.

He shook his head. "Not really. Well, is this off the record?"

"Yes, sir," Mickey said.

"Everybody else got theories," he said. "I'll give you mine. Either Wayne Williams got him and he was either never found or misidentified . . . or . . . my crazy-ass ex did something to him and is tryin' to cover it up. She keep attacking me so nobody suspect her."

They were interesting theories. He was a smart guy—and articulate. Why was he working as a short-order cook in the middle of the night?

"Tell you one thing," he said. "Whoever was behind it—her or someone else—did a damn good job of making the cops think it was me."

"How so?"

"Planted shit of his—clothes, toys and shit—in my car, my house. Convinced the cops he had been there, that I had him or had had him. Hell, if they hadn't been stretched so thin with the murders and if Vera had been a better mother, they wouldn't've left me alone."

The door opened and a trucker with an orange vest and brown baseball cap came in.

"I've got to get back to work," he said. "I appreciate y'all looking for my boy. Y'all find him, you let me know. Food's on the house tonight. Take care now."

As he moved away, back behind the counter, back to

his cooking station, I shook my head and looked at Mickey.

"What?" he said, meeting my eyes momentarily. "Your eyes are bulging out of your head. What is it?"

"What if the killer planted evidence on the dads to make the authorities think they had them to get them to stop looking?"

"Oh wow," he said. "That would be . . . wicked as fuck."

"We'll have to check with the others to confirm, and we still need to find the mothers, but if that's what it is . . ."

"It's ingenious," he said. "And it helped him get away with murder."

Chapter Thirty

Over the next few days, we tracked down as many of the fathers as we could—four of the six in all.

Interestingly, finding the mothers was proving far more difficult, but the fathers we found all told us the same story.

They didn't kidnap their sons and at some point someone placed something of their sons'—articles of clothing or other personal belongings—in their homes and vehicles.

Of the four dads we spoke with—Cedric's, Jamal's, Duke's, and Quentin's—all but Cedric's had the same exact experience.

"You know what this means?" Mickey said.

We were on 285 in heavy traffic, headed back toward Memorial Drive.

"What's that?"

"We're dealing with a serial killer. Wayne Williams or someone else—but that's what this is. Not fathers or other family members. Not runaways or kidnappings."

I didn't say anything, just thought about it.

"I've studied this type of killer a lot while working on my book," he said. "There's no motive—least none that we can ever understand. There are patterns. There are certain psychological signatures they leave, but . . . it's all fantasy driven for them. They're acting out some sick, horrific fantasy that involves sex and death."

I nodded.

"Scariest thing is how normal they can seem," he added. "I could be the killer, and you'd never know it."

"You don't seem that normal," I said.

He laughed.

I thought about the mask of humanity and sanity our killer might be wearing, and wondered what it might look like. Just how normal did he appear to be? How convincing was his disguise? How deeply buried was his surreal secret? Had we encountered him? Was he dead or in prison or in a psych ward somewhere? Was that why the murders stopped? Or had he just relocated? Were other people somewhere else unknowingly glancing at that mask, gazing day in and day out into an abyss that was gazing back, without even realizing that's what was happening?

"But seriously . . . we're not dealing with a human being here."

He was right, and I knew the things he was saying were true in themselves, but I questioned whether he was sensationalizing them for the sake of the story he was already crafting in his head.

"They have these extreme fantasies of sexual violence—starting in childhood or adolescence. Their isolation, compulsive behaviors, daydreaming, and increased acting out on animals and shit fuel their fantasies and eventually it all leads to murder—but not just one. A series. That's what we're dealing with here."

I nodded.

He waited a moment, then said, "You think it's the same killer?"

"Same killer as—"

"The Atlanta Child Murderer," he said. "The same one."

I shook my head. "If for no other reason than that the other killer dumped the bodies of his victims so they could be found relatively quickly and easily. In this case there are no bodies at all."

We had yet to track down Jaquez's and Vaughn's dads, and we were still having difficulty finding the moms, but we felt like we had enough to take to the police.

Lonnie let us use his storage/meeting room.

Frank Morgan, Bobby Battle, and Remy Boss, the original investigator of most of the cases, attended, and listened attentively as Mickey and I made our case.

We told them about the geographical connections between the victims, the similarity in the disappearances, and the way the killer had planted clothes and toys belonging to the victims in the dads' homes and vehicles.

When we finished, no one said anything at first.

I had expected hostility from Bobby Battle, but so far he had seemed quite sedate.

Eventually, Remy looked at Bobby and said, "Whatta you think?"

Bobby shrugged. "It was your case. You'd know better than any of us if there's even a possibility of it being true, but . . . I don't know . . . seems a little . . ."

Remy looked back at us. "I appreciate all the work you guys have done on this," he said. "And I'm not sayin' there's not something to it, but . . . the two biggest questions are the breakdowns in your pattern. Why wasn't anything planted on Cedric Porter's dad, and why is Vaughn Smith so far outside of your geographical area?"

"I have no idea," I said. "And I know we've yet to speak to Vaughn's or Jaquez's dad, but . . . We could be wrong about all this, but we thought it was enough to bring to you."

"It was," Remy said. "It is. You did the right thing. We'll look into it and see if we can find the other dads, make the other connections, answer the open questions."

"You still have the problem of no bodies," Battle said. "All this time and none of them have turned up. Argues against your serial killer theory. Williams dumped his in the woods and rivers and we found them pretty quick. If he did these, why haven't we found them? If someone else did, same question. Where are the bodies?"

"Again, I have no idea," I said. "I have far more questions than anything else—just felt like they were questions worth asking, ones y'all might want to try to answer."

"And we will," Remy said. "Thanks."

And that was that.

I didn't know exactly what I was expecting, but I felt an enormous letdown as we walked out of Lonnie's meeting room and into his video store.

Chapter Thirty-one

The four other men scattered quickly, each with pressing matters requiring their attention, and I was left standing there in the store that would soon be closed, looking around, but not seeing anything before me.

It wasn't until I realized Shaft and Foxy Brown, Lonnie's Bombay cats, were staring down at me from the top of the shelf I was standing in front of that I came back to the present time and place.

"You okay?" Lonnie asked.

I nodded. "Thanks for letting us use your room."

"No problem. Happy to help. How'd it go?"

I told him.

"For what it's worth, I think you're right," he said.

"Thanks."

"I'm not just sayin' that," he said. "It makes a certain sense like nothin' else ever has. If the cops drop the ball on this again . . . I'll hire someone . . . private. Not going to my grave without knowing what happened to Cedric. I can't."

I nodded. "How are you doing?"

He shrugged. "Feeling weak . . . like . . . I . . . I've been tempted to start drinkin' again."

"I'm sorry to hear that. Anything I can do to help?"

He shook his head. "Got a good sponsor. He's

helpin'. I'll call him before I . . . do anything too stupid."

"Do."

"I will," he said. "Will you do something for me?"

"What's that?"

"Don't stop looking for Cedric," he said. "Don't leave it up to them."

I didn't say anything, just thought about it.

"Think about how much time they've had," he said. "And they wouldn't have anything new now if it weren't for you."

I nodded. He was right.

"Thing is, I've got nothin' left," he said. "I'll be losing my store soon. Have no idea what I'm gonna do next. But I'll spend every last cent of my savings to find Cedric. And truth is . . . I'd like to get to whoever took him before the police do—not that they ever will."

I thought about what he had done to Daryl Lee Gibbons and Cedric Porter, Sr., and knew exactly what he would do to the man who had taken his surrogate son.

When I stepped out of Lonnie's shop, I saw Frank Morgan in his car out in the parking lot not far from the phone booth I had used to call him last week.

He motioned me over.

When I reached his car, I could see that he was on his radio so I waited, watching the traffic on Memorial, the activity on the sidewalks and shops.

The wind was more biting today, and I shoved my hands in my pants pockets.

When Frank finished, he climbed out of the car and closed the door.

"How well do you know Mickey?" he asked.

"Not well at all. Why?"

"His name rang a bell, and when you said he was a reporter I remembered something about a scandal he was involved in. I called a newsman friend of mine to make sure. He used to write under the name Michael Davis. Switched to Mickey after he got fired from the *Journal*. You need to be careful with him."

"Okay," I said. "I have been, but why?"

"He was fired for manufacturing a story, making up quotes from sources, in some cases making up the sources themselves. If he'll do that for a newspaper story, imagine what he'll do for his book."

I nodded.

"Did anything we went over in there come only from him?" he asked.

I thought about it.

"No," I said. "Best I can recall, the only thing that has come from him during the entire course of the investigation and our group meeting is that Daryl Lee Gibbons has a record."

"Which is true. He does. Think I'm pretty close to finding him, by the way. We'll see what he's been up to and what he has to say about what happened back then."

"Great. Thanks."

"Just be careful, John. I don't trust this Michael Mickey Davis character. I don't think you should either. Think he's got a very different motive than you do, has an agenda, and it's selfish and sensational and can only hurt the investigation."

Chapter Thirty-two

When I pulled back the curtains and looked out, I saw Summer Grantham standing there, her blond hair up in a ponytail, her eyes looking far sadder than I had seen before.

I had been alone in my room studying the cases, hoping she might come by.

I nodded toward my front door, and met her at it to let her in.

"Sorry," she said.

"For what?"

"Just showing up like this. Not calling or coming by before now. You name it, I'm sorry for it."

"Come in. Are you okay?"

We embraced for a few moments, then I led her down the hallway to my room and closed the door behind us.

"What's going on?" I asked. "Where have you been? Why did you disappear? What's wrong?"

She frowned and her eyes glistened. "Can we not talk about it right now?"

"I'd really like to," I said, "but . . . if you can't . . ."

"In a little while maybe," she said. "Okay?"

"Okay."

"How have you been?" she asked.

"Besides worried about you and wondering what the hell happened to you? Pretty fair. You?"

"Not so good. I'm sorry again."

"Could I at least get your number and address so I can contact you? You're not listed."

She shook her head. "It's under my husband's name."

"Your *what?*"

"I know. I'm sorry. I should've—"

"Let me walk you to the door," I said.

"Wait. Sorry. I meant ex-husband. We're not married anymore. I just never changed it over to my name."

"So you'll give me the number?" I said. "We can go there right now? We can go see your ex and he'll tell me he's in fact your ex?"

She nodded, then gave me her phone number and address though I had nothing to write them down on at the moment.

"All but the visit him part," she said. "He's in prison."

"I'm not sure I believe you, Summer," I said. "I'm not sure I believe anything you're saying—or have said to me."

She nodded, tears beginning to stream now.

"I don't blame you," she said, "but it is the truth. Everything I've ever told you is. The only thing I've done is not tell you one thing—a very big thing, but that's it."

"What's the big thing?"

"I suffer from depression," she said. "It goes along with the gift. My grandmother who also had the gift battled with the same dark demon. That's where I've been. I haven't gotten out of bed in nearly a week."

I believed her.

To the best of my ability to discern deception, I sincerely believed she was telling me the truth.

Everything in me wanted to take care of her, to hug and reassure her, to help her fight the darkness she was dealing with.

"I believe you," I said.

"You do?"

"I do. And I want to help you."

"You do?"

"I do," I said. "But I can't."

"What?"

"Are you on medication?" I asked.

She nodded.

"Are you taking it?"

She nodded again.

"Are you under a doctor's or psychiatrist's care?"

She nodded again.

"Do you have a family member or friend who can help you?"

She nodded. "My daughter. She's . . . very good at helping me deal."

"Does she know how you're doing right now?"

She nodded again. "I'm actually much better now," she said. "She knew how I was earlier in the week. She checked on me every day."

"Good," I said. "Then . . . since you have all that, I'll walk you to the door. I'm sorry. I wish I could help you—I mean, I don't even know if you wanted me to help— but I just can't. I want to. You can't imagine how much everything in me wants to. But I just did that with another woman—it's sort of my thing, I guess—and it didn't go well at all. So . . . I'm truly trying to accept the things I cannot change and change the things I can."

"That's good," she said. "That's very good."

We walked back down the hallway in silence.

When we reached the front door, we stopped.

"I didn't come here tonight looking for you to save me, John," she said. "At least the best part of me didn't. I just wanted to explain and to . . . I wanted to be close again, maybe have some of the healing that flowed through me to you, flow back through you to me, but . . . we knew what this was, what the other night was. I'm more than twice your age. My daughter is a good bit older than you. But here's the thing . . . what it was was sacred. What it was was real. What we shared, this connection, this . . . Don't lose that, don't let your aversion to drama and messiness, which I understand and appreciate, cause you to close down again and miss out on what life has for you."

I nodded.

She kissed me quickly, then turned to leave.

"Wait," I said.

She stopped.

When she turned I saw hope and desire in her eyes, and regretted calling out to her.

"Sorry," I said. "I wasn't trying to . . . I just want to walk you to your car."

I *could be in bed with Summer right now.*

Had I made the wrong decision? Was I being too cautious, too rigid, too—

I decided to occupy my mind with something else.

Thinking back to my conversation with Mickey earlier in the day, I turned my attention to the type of motiveless murderer we might be pursuing.

A compulsive or serial or ritual killer—I wasn't completely sure I understood the difference—is a killer who kills two or more people for psychological gratification. The murders must take place over more than a month and include a cooling off period between them. Most often the murders involve a sexual component and are carried out in a similar manner on victims who have certain commonalities—such as age, race, body type, or sex.

Serial or compulsive killers are often psychopaths or display the psychopathic traits such as sensation seeking, lacking guilt or remorse, predatory actions, impulsivity, and the need to control. In contrast with people with other major mental disorders such as schizophrenia, psychopaths can seem normal and can often be quite charming.

These type killers are often the victims of childhood abuse—emotional, physical, or sexual—often by a family member. Because of this, serial killers typically programed as children to become murderers by progressively intensifying a dark loop of dangerous, violent fantasies—elaborate mental thoughts with great preoccupation anchored in the daydreaming process. These fantasies serve to relieve anxiety, stress, tension, and fear—transforming the normal fantasies of childhood into a dangerous, compulsive form of escapism to deal with their isolation, pain, fear, abuse, neglect, and trauma.

When these dark, violent fantasies are combined with compulsive masturbation, a sexual component is added to the cognitive or mental process.

Anger, isolation, and resentment fuel fantasies, which leads to further isolation, which leads to an even greater reliance on fantasy for pleasure and relief from anxiety.

By the time a serial killer claims his first victim, he has fantasized, planned, plotted, obsessed over every minute detail of it for years. At a certain point, fantasy is no longer enough, and the killer reaches a state where he actually wants to live out his dark, violent daydreams. At this stage his victim is reduced to a mere player in the serial killer's mind movie of sex and murder.

After committing his first murder, the novice killer will obsess over his need to kill again. Having discovered the key to acting out his secret desires, some killers continue to murder in order to experience the fantasy again and again, while others grow bored and move to escalate their actions instead.

All this—all this horrific death and devastation born out of the daydreams of a weak, frightened, terrorized little child.

Could it be that a victimized child, now housed in the body of an adult, was making victims of other children?

Chapter Thirty-three

I saw Summer the next day.

We were both back at Safe Haven for our next group meeting.

She seemed sad, but not overly so.

I came in a few minutes late and sat in the only seat left in the small circle, which put me directly across from her.

I nodded and gave her a small smile.

She returned it.

Over her shoulder, as if it were a month or so ago, as if he were still there, I caught a glimpse of Martin Fisher coloring at the small table—just like he had been the last night we were here together.

I blinked and he was gone, but I could still feel him, still sense his presence in the room that had held so many children over the years.

"I don't think we're doing enough for Wayne Williams," Annie Bowers, the thin, black woman from the Free Wayne Williams initiative, said. "I know that everything we do is important, but . . . it seems to me that . . . well, there's only so much we can do for victims who are already deceased. But Wayne is still alive. What we do for him . . . can make a real difference."

Miss Ida cleared her throat. "Our group has no agenda," she said. "Not that one or any other. It can't. We're not here to free Wayne Williams. We're here to share information and ideas and do a little investigating where we can. If that leads to Wayne Williams being released, so be it. If it proves his guilt beyond a reasonable doubt, so be it. What we do here—not forgetting him, caring about him and his case, seeking some kind of imperfect justice, which is the only kind we get in this world—is a worthy endeavor, a noble cause. That helps me and it helps us. Sure, it won't bring him back, but does make sure he's not forgotten."

It was the most eloquent I had ever heard Miss Ida be.

"I understand what you're saying, I do," Annie said. "I'm just saying . . . we could save an innocent man."

"Lot of us don't think he is innocent," Melvin Pryor said. "Others aren't sure. We're here for the victims."

"That's what I'm saying," she said. "He *is* a victim of this terrible tragedy, a living victim, spending every day of his life confined for something he didn't do."

"If that's true," Preston Mailer, the ex-cop said, "then maybe the work we do will help free him. Maybe it will."

"Just be clear on why we're here," Ida said. "We don't mind that you have an agenda, but our group does not and cannot."

Annie nodded. "I understand. I don't agree, but I understand."

"John? Mickey?" Ida said. "Want to share with us what you've been doing?"

"Sure," I said. "We've talked with Cedric's father. Jamal's too. We've looked into whether the missing kids on our new list are just with their dads, like the police believe, or if something else is going on. We think something else is going on."

"Why?" Mailer asked.

I told them, with Mickey tossing in a detail or two along the way.

"So if the dads don't have them . . ." Rose Lee said.

"If they're still alive it would go a long way toward proving Wayne's innocence," Annie Bowers said.

No one responded to that.

"I had an idea," I said. "Wondered if you thought Ada Baker would go for it."

"What's that?" Ida asked.

"Tapping her phone and tracing the next call she gets from Cedric or whoever's calling her."

Ida shook her head.

"That was mentioned initially, but she said she feared for Cedric's safety, that he had to have a good reason for running and hiding and she didn't want him found until he wanted to be."

I thought about that.

"Calling her like that is such torture," Summer said. "Wonder who's doing it and why?"

They were the most words she had spoken in any of the groups.

"You don't think it's Cedric?" I asked.

She shrugged. "It's torture either way."

"We should ask her again," Mickey said. "If we can trace the call . . . we can find out what the hell is goin' on."

"I'll talk to her again," Ida said. "But don't expect much. Don't think she's likely to change her mind."

"**H**ow are you?" I asked.

Summer and I were standing beneath the covered

walkway, lingering to speak to one another as the others were leaving.

"Better," she said.

"Good."

"Sorry again," she said. "For my baggage. Can't be helped. Would if it could. That Serenity Prayer thing you mentioned, I practice it too. I'm changing everything I can, everything I'm capable of."

I nodded. "Don't doubt that for a second."

Be kind. I thought of the quote most often attributed to Plato. *Everyone you meet is fighting a hard battle.*

"Sorry again for the hard line of the boundaries I have to set right now," I said. "I wouldn't if they weren't necessary."

"I know. Believe me, I get it."

"Hey," Miss Ida called to us. "You two feel like taking a ride?"

She was walking back toward us from the parking lot.

We began moving toward her.

"I'm goin' to talk to Ada now," she said. "Y'all want to go?"

I nodded and looked at Summer.

She shrugged. "Is it okay?"

"Sure, honey," Ida said, "I wouldn't've—oh. You meant with . . ."

"Of course," I said.

"No way," Ada said. "No way I do that to my boy. Done enough to him already."

"But it would help us find him," Ida said.

"He don't want to be found," she said. "I got to honor that. He'a come home when he ready."

"What if he can't?" I said. "What if he's being held hostage? What if they let him call as a way of controlling him, but he can't tell you what he really wants to?"

She thought about that as if it hadn't occurred to her before.

After a while, she slowly began shaking her head. "Just can't. Don't trust the po-lice to . . . Too much can go wrong."

A thought occurred to me.

"What if we hired a private firm to do it?" I said. "What if they only told you and one other person you trust? Miss Ida. Lonnie. It'd be up to you. You could then do with the information what you wanted."

"Hmm. Let me think about that one," she said.

"It's a real chance of finding him, Ada," Ida said. "It was me, I'd take it."

"What if it the wrong thing, Miss Ida? What if it harm him somehow? I'd rather him be safe without me than . . . anything happen to him 'cause I tryin' to get him back."

"I didn't sense any deception in anything she said," Summer said.

She, Ida, and I were standing out in the parking lot in front of Ada's building.

The night was cold and windy, and we wouldn't be standing here long.

"Not like I did the last time I was here," she added.

"Whatcha mean, girl?" Ida said.

"She wasn't being totally truthful about where she was between the time Cedric left the apartment and when she arrived at Scarlett's."

"Oh, yeah, that," Ida said. "Always assumed she was turning a trick or scoring some dope—probably both, the one for the other. Wouldn't mean she had anything to do with what happened to Cedric."

"Except because of neglect," Summer said.

"You probably right," Ida said, "but take it from a mother who was overprotective of her boy, you only have to turn your back for a second and . . ."

LaMarcus playing in his backyard, just a few feet away from the watchful eyes of his mother and sister. There one minute, gone the next, his body found in a large culvert in a drainage ditch later that night. He had looked like he was sleeping. That sleep of death and what dreams may come that followed it had flung his mother into a wakeful nightmare of the cruelest kind.

When I walked into the apartment, my phone was ringing.

It was Frank Morgan.

"Approval came through, he said. "Everything's set. You see him tomorrow."

Nothing else need be said. I knew who the *he* was. I would spend the rest of the sleepless night thinking about my second encounter with the man who obsessed my waking hours, the monster who had haunted my dreams.

Chapter Thirty-four

"**W**hat're you hoping to get out of this?" Frank asked.

I shrugged. "I don't know."

What I did know was that I wasn't ready, wasn't prepared, and I didn't know how to be.

We were sitting in a hallway outside the conference room in the Admin building, waiting on Wayne Williams to arrive.

"Is there something in particular you want to ask him?" he said.

I shook my head. "Just want to look into his eyes."

"Well, now's your chance," he said. "Here he comes."

Two correctional officers escorted Wayne Williams into the building. He was neither cuffed nor shackled, and he looked to be out on a casual stroll.

We stood.

When he reached us, he extended his hand and we each shook it and spoke to him.

"Thank you for agreeing to do this, Mr. Williams," Frank said. "The GBI really appreciates it."

"No problem," he said. "Happy to help if I can."

"Right in here," one of the COs said, motioning us toward the Admin conference room.

"I'll be here if you need me," Frank said. "Just yell."

He then sat back down on the sofa, and Williams and I walked into the conference room.

I don't know exactly what I was expecting, but it wasn't this—not something as innocuous as a conference room. I had pictured either a small, empty room with two metal chairs and a metal table, Williams's cuffs and shackles chained to a hook in the concrete floor. Or a visiting booth with a plexiglass partition, each of us communicating through a telephone receiver.

A conversation in a conference room between two guys—neither of whom were cuffed or armed—was just so . . . pedestrian.

The COs remained outside with Frank. The door closed, and I was alone with Wayne Williams.

I wanted to look into his eyes, and I did. I locked on to them and didn't avert my gaze—even when I wanted to.

The eyes I looked into were hooded and blinked a lot behind large glasses.

He was smaller than I remembered, had lost some of the soft roundness in his face and pudginess around his midsection. He no longer had an afro, and his close-cropped hair appeared to be beginning to recede a bit.

Could this really be the monster who had left such a wide wake of devastation behind him, haunted my childhood, changed the course of my life?

"Do you remember me?" I asked.

He canted his head slightly and narrowed his eyes. Lifting his hand, partially pointing a finger at me as if it was coming to him. "I might . . ." he said. "You look familiar. Help me out."

"I was twelve. You were twenty-two. We met in the arcade at the Omni. You were passin' out flyers."

"Oh, yeah," he said. "I do remember. I knew you

looked familiar."

He didn't recognize or remember me. He was a compulsive and accomplished liar. I knew that already.

I was now eighteen and he was twenty-eight, the six years between our first encounter and this one compressing the age difference separating us down to a point of nearly nonexistence. We were both adults now.

"Agent Morgan mentioned you're a theology student," he said.

I nodded.

"And you also have an interest in criminal investigation?"

"I do."

"You ever thought of working in a place like this?" he said. "Prison chaplain can do a lot of good."

I shook my head. "That's interesting. No, I never have."

"You should consider it," he said. "You could minister to the spiritual needs of the inmate population and reexamine the cases of those who claim to be innocent."

"You still maintain your innocence, don't you?" I said.

"I don't just maintain my innocence. I *am* innocent. Nobody will tell you they saw Wayne Williams kill another person, hit another person, stab another person, shoot another person, choke another person, or hurt another person in any way."

I knew that to be true. Not a single eyewitness ever came forward to say they had seen him hurt or kill anyone. There were witnesses who placed him with some of the victims, but that was it.

"Why do you think you were convicted?" I asked.

"Honestly? Let me tell you. The city of Atlanta was ready to explode. They had to have a scapegoat and he

had to be black. That was me. Now look, yes, I was my
own worst enemy—goin' off on the stand like that. I did
a lot of stupid stuff. I was just a buzz-headed kid, but that
doesn't make me a killer, does it?"

I shook my head. "No, it doesn't."

We were quiet a moment.

I tried to get a sense of the man sitting across from
me. He was really difficult to read. But there was something
about him, more an absence of something than a presence.
I was having a hard time determining exactly what it was.

"If it wasn't you, do you have any ideas on who the
murderer was?" I asked.

"Well, look, yes, I have some theories, but that's all
they are. I don't have any knowledge of anything. I wasn't a
witness to anything. I will say this—it wasn't just one killer.
Some may've been the Klan, some parents or relatives,
some some kind of sex ring—older men messin' around
with some drop shot kids gettin' paid for sex acts."

"You know a lot about your case," I said. "I'm sure
you've studied a lot of others like it, probably know far
more than most about these kinds of things."

"Unfortunately, I guess I do."

"If there were a series of similar murders—young
boys like so many of the victims in the missing and
murdered children case—but no bodies were ever found,
why do you think that would be?"

"How many we talking?"

"Not sure. Say six or more."

"Well, now, no body no murder," he said. "No
evidence. Missing kids cases don't get much attention, but a
murdered kid . . ."

I nodded. "But how could the killer keep the bodies
from being discovered?"

"Think about the clown killer from Chicago," he

said. "Gacy. Hid the bodies right in his house. Serves another purpose too. Keeps them close. Don't have to give them up when you're . . ."

I thought about it.

"Or he could just be buryin' them in a place no one has looked yet," he said. "Woods. Foundation at a construction site. Graveyard. Crematorium. What if there's nothing left of them because he used acid or something like that?"

"Can you explain why you failed a polygraph?" I said.

Actually, he had failed three.

"Well, now, yes, I think . . . I believe I can. Some people . . . those tests aren't a certain science, not one hundred percent accurate. Some people can pass 'em and others fail 'em no matter what. Just one of those things."

Just one of those things.

"What about Cheryl Johnson?" I asked.

She was the woman he claimed he was supposed to meet the morning after his arrest. Said he was out looking for her address the night he was stopped on the bridge. All this time and she had never come forward. One of the biggest, most high profile cases in history and she didn't hear about it, didn't know everyone was looking for her? None of her friends or family members stepped forward and even asked if it could be her?

He gave me a half frown with a small smile peeking out behind it. "I have no answer for that. She probably just didn't want to get involved. Maybe it was a prank from the beginning. Maybe somebody was trying to set me up—and it worked."

There were so many things I wanted to ask him and we were running out of time.

What do I ask? What can I say to get him to reveal something new, something that would help with the case? Think. Come on. You don't have long.

"There were reports that you and your dad burned all kinds of items—documents, pictures, clothing, things like that—after you became a suspect. What did you burn and why?"

"It was just trash," he said. "Nothing more. Nothing sinister. I can see how it would look, but at the time . . . I just didn't think about it."

You're lying.

"How do you explain all the trace evidence connecting you to so many of the victims?" I asked.

He shrugged. "Look, I was set up. I don't know by who or what all they did, but they did enough to make it happen, right? Fake a phone call from somebody claiming to be Cheryl Johnson. Manufacture evidence. Hide evidence of other suspects. Hide evidence that contradicts the story they're weaving. I don't know. I just know Wayne Williams is innocent and no eyewitness says otherwise."

Chapter Thirty-five

"**W**ell?" Frank asked.

He had waited until we were back in his car, a GBI-issued boxy navy-blue Ford LTD, to say anything.

It was raining when we walked out of Georgia State Prison near Reidsville, a cold, hard rain that turned the late afternoon gunmetal gray and pelted us as we ran toward the vehicle.

The same hard rain was now pelting the car as we drove up I-16 toward Macon.

I shrugged.

"Not ready to talk about it?" he said.

"I'm not sure what I think," I said. "Or feel. It was very interesting—and I got to do what I wanted to do. I looked into his eyes."

"Did you see his soul?"

"I didn't."

"That's because he doesn't have one," he said.

Though on high, the wipers couldn't keep up with the water sluicing down the windshield, but traffic was light and Frank drove like he was ready to be home.

"I just feel like I . . . like it was a missed opportunity," I said.

He let out a little burst of laughter.

"'Cause you didn't get him to confess?" he said.

I smiled. "Yeah maybe. I don't know. I just . . ."

"It's all about expectation," he said. "You went in there thinkin' you were actually goin' to get him to confess or prove to you his innocence."

"I'm not so sure it was like that, but I did want to gain something, learn something new, something to justify the time and effort you put into making it happen."

"You probably got far more out of it than you know," he said. "I wouldn't be surprised if things he said didn't keep coming to you for a while. I get you—"

His pager vibrated at the same time dispatch called for him on his radio.

He radioed in and was informed that a last known address had been located for Daryl Lee Gibbons. It was on Old Conyers Road near Stockbridge. Daryl Lee and his mother were believed to be renting a basement apartment from an elderly couple.

"I'll try to swing by and pay a visit to ol' Daryl Lee tomorrow," he said.

"Or," I said, "we could swing by tonight. We'll be coming in on 75. It'd only be ten minutes or so out of our way."

"Do you know what you see when you look up the word *relentless* in the dictionary?" he said.

"A picture of me?"

"No, the definition of relentless. And do you know what it says after that?"

"No, what?"

"See also John Jordan."

"Is that a no?" I asked.

"No, it's not a no."

The house was a split-level ranch–style built on a
hill—one story showing in the front, two in the back. It
was made of beige brick and had a swimming pool behind
it.

Though it was around eight in the evening when we
arrived, the house was completely dark and there were no
signs anyone was home.

The sweep of Frank's headlights as we pulled in
to the circular drive showed a once nice home now in
disrepair, a yard in need of maintenance, and a car with two
flat tires that looked abandoned.

"Doesn't look like anyone's home," Frank said.

"Or that anyone lives here any longer," I said.

"It was just a last known," he said. "They could've
moved on long ago. But we're here, so let's knock on the
door."

We did.

Then we banged.

Eventually we heard movement inside.

And a while after that, an obese middle-aged woman
with very bad teeth appeared in the darkness through the
partially opened door.

Frank flashed his badge.

"Georgia Bureau of Investigation," he said. "You
are?"

"Mrs. Tilda Gibbons."

"We need to speak to your son, Mrs. Gibbons."

"He ain't here."

"Then we'll speak to you," he said. "Turn on some
lights and let us in."

"Lights been shut off," she said. "Come back
tomorrow."

Frank pulled out a small flashlight that looked like a

thick writing pen and shone it in the woman's face.

"Where are Mr. and Mrs. Ward?"

"Who?"

"The owners of this home?"

"Oh, them. They moved to Florida."

While she was still speaking, he pushed on the door and stepped inside.

I followed.

She stumbled backward, gasping and grunting as she did.

In the small spill of Frank's tiny light, I could see a once elegant, if outdated home, filled with filth and crammed with clutter.

We hadn't made it very far into the foyer when the odor hit us—a complex, layered reek of rotting food, competing fruity air-freshener flavors, dust and decay, body odor, and the unmistakable sickly sweet stench of death.

Frank drew his weapon.

Chapter Thirty-six

"Why does it smell like someone died in here?" Frank asked.

"Our old cat," she said. "Crawled up in some small space and died. We can't find it. That's all. Come back tomorrow when there's light. Daryl Lee be home by then."

"Come in here and have a seat," he said, motioning her toward the den with his light.

We followed her through the foyer and stepped down into a shag-carpeted den with a fireplace, an enormous old dark wooden cabinet console television, and custom bookshelves that filled an entire wall.

"Sit," Frank said.

"I ain't no dog," Tilda Gibbons said, but plopped down onto the green vinyl sofa along the wall across from the fireplace, nearly eclipsing it as she did.

"John, I need you to go to the car and radio for backup," he said. "Explain the situation as best you can. Have them call Clayton County Sheriffs in. Oh, and tell them we need lights."

He shone his light at me and tossed me the keys, but I was unable to see them because of the light and they bounced off the side of my arm and fell to the floor. He shone the light on the floor until he found them, then I grabbed them and rushed out to make the transmission.

I was gone for maybe five minutes.

When I got back in, Frank was standing in the doorway between the den and kitchen, alternating between keeping an eye on Tilda Gibbons and sweeping the kitchen with his light.

"They're on the way," I said. "Should only be a few minutes."

"I should've had you grab my flashlight out of the trunk," he said.

"Want me to go—"

From somewhere in the house, we heard a child yell and begin to cry.

"Where's that coming from?" Frank asked.

I strained to hear.

Suddenly Tilda Gibbons erupted from the couch and screamed, "Daryl Lee, cops are here!"

She then began moving toward the hallway on the opposite end of the room from where we stood, which led to what looked to be about four closed doors.

We both began to run after her, but Frank held out his arm and said, "Stay behind me."

I did.

At the end of the hallway was a large window.

Tilda Gibbons never slowed.

Running as fast as her size would allow, she dove through the window, splintering the wood frame and shattering the panes of glass.

When we reached it and looked down, the wind blowing the bullet-like raindrops through the open hole in the house, we could see that she had fallen two stories down to a second driveway leading to a two-car garage below.

The fall had not killed her.

She lay there moaning, splayed out, unable to move, the halo of blood around her head turning pink in the thumping rain.

"Listen," Frank said. "We've got to find that kid."

We followed the sounds back down the hallway.

"Let's just try all the doors," he said.

I grabbed the knob of the door closest to me, turned it, and pushed. It was unlocked and gave a little, but something on the floor kept it from opening all the way. I shoved harder, and it gave a little more. Using my foot at the bottom, I pushed again.

Death was on the other side of the door. I could smell it.

"This one's clear," Frank said.

"Need your light," I said. "Got a bad one."

I had the door open enough to squeeze inside, and could see that a towel at the bottom was what had been impeding my progress. It was obviously there to block the smell from coming out beneath the door.

Easing in, I stood there a moment and waited for Frank to arrive with the light. He handed it to me and I scanned the room.

Beneath a ceiling fan, each blade of which was covered with hanging car deodorizers, an elderly couple, Mr. and Mrs. Ward was my guess, were dead in their bed, their bodies in an advanced state of decay.

Coughing and gagging and suppressing the vomit at the back of my throat, I shoved my way back through the door and closed it behind me.

When I was sure I wasn't going to throw up, I told Frank what I had seen.

"You okay?" he asked. "Two more doors."

"Yeah," I said, and reached for the next door.

It was locked.

Taking a couple of steps back toward the center of the hallway, I lowered my shoulder and jumped into the door.

It gave and I tumbled inside. The faint light from a distant streetlamp streamed in through the small window and illuminated the tiny room.

It was a bathroom.

There in a sunken tub, a small, naked, thin white boy of about five lay on a blanket soiled with his own urine, feces, and blood.

Chapter Thirty-seven

He was no longer crying, but he was alive.

"Frank," I yelled.

Reaching down, I lifted the child. I had the urge to cover his nakedness with the blanket, but it was far too foul.

"It's okay," I whispered. "I've got you. You're safe."

Frank appeared at the door.

"Oh dear God," he said.

I blinked back tears as a memory mosaic of Martin Fisher formed in my mind. I had been too late to help him, but not this little fella.

Of course, that was only partially true. In a very real sense we were too late. Way too late.

"Find him," I said. "Find him and put him down. Or give me your gun and let me do it."

A sound came from the kitchen and Frank turned toward it.

"Take the boy outside and wait for the Clayton County Sheriffs to arrive," he said. He then ran down the hallway, chasing the small beam of his light through the den and into the kitchen.

As soon as he entered the kitchen there were two quick flashes of light, two loud explosions. Shotgun bursts.

Followed by Frank falling to the floor.

I tried to set the child down on the couch, but he would not let go.

Clinging to him, I ran over to the kitchen and peeked in, using the cabinets near the door for cover.

Frank was on the floor, blood blooming out around him, his .45 still in his hand.

Crouching down, I leaned in just beyond the bottom cabinet and looked around.

There was no sign of Daryl Lee Gibbons. There was an open door on the other end leading into darkness.

With the boy still clinging to me, I leaned in, grabbed Frank's ankle, and began pulling him toward the den.

I could hear Daryl Lee Gibbons running down the stairs to the basement, so I moved in to get a better grip on Frank, grabbing his gun and checking for signs of life as I did.

Then footfalls. Running. Fast. Toward us.

Standing, turning, bringing up the gun, I could see Creepy Daryl Lee Gibbons running toward us, his shoulders lowered like he was going to tackle us.

I squeezed off a round of Frank's .45.

The boy screamed.

Then we were hit. Hard. At the legs.

Up. Airborne. Flying. Floating.

Clinging to the kid.

Banging into the window, breaking boards and glass, flying through the cold, wet, air, raindrops hitting us like scattershot.

Falling, flailing, trying to find purchase on anything.

Nothing.

Crab-crawling through the night air.

Two stories down.

Then hard, wet hit.

Sinking.

I had landed on my back on the pool cover.

Cold rain. Colder pool water.

Breath knocked out of me. Sucking air that wasn't there.

Cover collapsing onto us, sinking into the freezing dark wetness, still holding on to the small child who was no longer holding on back.

Corner of my eye, cement pad around the pool, very edge, Creepy Daryl Lee Gibbons facedown, unmoving, rain falling crimson around him.

I tried to stand, to swim, to do anything but sink, but sink was all I could do. I was wrapped in the mesh pool cover, unable to move in any meaningful way, unable to do anything but lift the child, try to hold him above the water for as long as I could.

So cold. So dark. So deep.

Sinking.

Submerged.

Engulfed.

Then . . . miraculously . . . rising.

Up out of the water.

Turning my head, I could see two Clayton County sheriff's deputies, one on each side of the pool, lifting the cover and us with it, out of the water and up into the night rain.

Chapter Thirty-eight

The boy, whose name was Bradley, had been abducted from the Kroger grocery market in Stockbridge a few days before.

His mom had an altercation with a fat woman matching Tilda Gibbons's description, and when she turned back around, Bradley was gone.

He was going to be okay—in one way. In many others he was not, and would not ever be.

He was taken to Henry General Hospital. His mom had been waiting for him there, and there was no doctor, nurse, or authority on heaven or earth that could make her leave his side—even if she had to scrub in for any procedures he needed.

There were two other children missing in the area, and crime scene techs were taking apart the house on Old Conyers right now, hoping they had been taken by family members instead of Creepy Gibbons and his pederast-enabling mother.

I was interviewed by a detective with the Clayton County Sheriff's Department and an agent with GBI, going over every detail of every second since we left Georgia State Prison earlier in the afternoon.

I had been allowed to dry off and change into some

extra sweats they had, and though I had a blanket draped around me and the heat was on in the interview room, I still shivered.

After about two hours, Tommy Daughtry, the sheriff, walked in.

He was a tall, thick man with a bit of a belly. He wore cowboy boots and a hat, and talked with one of the thicker Southern accents I had heard in a while.

"Far as I'm concerned, you're a hero," he said. "A goddamn hero. You and Agent Morgan."

"How is he?"

Frank had been airlifted to Grady Memorial and rushed into surgery.

"No word yet," he said.

"I'd like to go see him," I said. "Least be there when he comes out of surgery. Is there anybody here who can give me a ride to my car?"

"I'll do it myself," he said. "But there's something you should know."

"What's that?"

"They took those two sick, fat fuckers there too."

"The Gibbons's? They're alive?"

"Unfortunately."

We all took a moment to let that sink in.

"I don't have to worry about you finishing what you started, do I?" he said.

"I didn't start anything to finish," I said. "Both of their injuries are self-inflicted."

"Kiddy diddlers like them," the detective said, "won't last long in prison."

"You're being a bit too optimistic," the sheriff said. "I'm hoping they don't make it out of surgery."

When I was dropped off at my car, I drove directly to Trade Winds, the apartment complex I had lived in until a month or so back, the one where Jordan, Martin, and I had been a family of sorts.

Parking near the basketball court where Martin and I had spent so much time together, I got out and walked over to it in the driving rain.

I hadn't been dry long and now I was getting soaked through all over again.

I didn't care.

I stood beneath the goal where Martin had worked so hard to master the art of the layup, his smallness just too big an impediment.

In the darkness, the rain water looked like blood on the court, puddling black beneath the rain in the nearly nonexistent moonlight.

Dropping to the asphalt, I broke down and began to weep.

I wept for the world, for Martin and Jordan, for Cedric and Bradley, for all the childless mothers, for all the boys who would never grow to be men, but most of all, selfishly, I wept for me—for what I had once had and now had no longer.

Like the vanishing of everything else that had been lost, my tears disappeared into the falling rain so fast it was as if I weren't crying at all.

But I was.

I knew it.

The rain knew it.

And maybe, just maybe, somewhere in the wide, wide world, Martin and Jordan knew it too.

Later that night, back in my bedroom, I thought about the six missing boys I was looking for—not as missing or potentially murdered, not as victims, but as boys.

Holding Bradley the way I had tonight had really gotten to me, and I wanted to think of the boys I was looking for not as parts of a case, but as the vibrant, idiosyncratic little human beings they were—or had been that last time they were seen.

Cedric Porter, Jamal Jackson, Quentin Washington, Jaquez Anderson, Duke Ellis, and Vaughn Smith.

Jamal was a little jokester, always smiling, laughing, kidding around. Quentin was quiet—a large, mostly silent boy who had an inner strength that was obvious to everyone. Cedric and Vaughn loved movies, would watch them all the time if allowed. Duke adored football. He liked all sports, but adored football and could tell you every single statistic about his favorite players and teams. Jaquez, truly an Atlanta boy, loved all the Atlanta teams and followed them the way only a hometown fan can. Just ask him anything about the Hawks, the Falcons, or the Braves. He could tell you.

These were children, each one a little bundle of life and potential, each one innocent of what befell him.

Bradley was back with his mom.

Now let's see what we can do about getting the others back home with theirs.

"Sorry to call so late," Ida Williams said when I answered the phone, "but you don't sleep anyway, right?"

"Right."

"Were you asleep?"

"I wasn't," I said.

"What's wrong? You don't sound so good."

"Just tired. How are you?"

"I'm okay, son," she said. "Considering everything, I'm okay. Callin' 'cause I had a thought."

"Let's hear it."

"Mickey said y'all's havin' a hard time locating the mothers of the victims from over there."

"Yeah, I think he is."

"Before I tell you my thought, let me tell you somethin' else."

"Okay."

"Ain't no relationship in the world like that of a black mother and her son," she said.

I knew that to be true—and not just from what I had read, but what I had seen firsthand. I thought of my best friend back home, Merrill, and his mother, Mama Monroe, and the ferocious way she mothered him.

"A Southern black woman in America knows all too well what she doin' when she brings a black male child into this world, into this country, into the part of the country where we live. Our boys will always be perceived as a threat, always eyed with suspicion, always viewed as less than. Many of our boys never get to grow up."

I thought of her son LaMarcus, who had died as a child.

"If they do," she continued, "they seen as even more of a menace, even more of a threat. Live half-lives on borrowed time. Never know which day it be they don't come home. Get gunned down, arrested. This makes them extra special to us, makes us love them and care for them in a way we don't anyone else. Probably ain't all that good for 'em, but you can see why we do it—baby 'em, spoil 'em. What else can we do?"

"I understand."

I thought about something James Baldwin wrote. *A black mama's instinct is to protect the black male from the devastation that threatens him the moment he declares himself a man.*

Ida was saying it began long before he declared himself a man, and she was right.

But it wasn't just black mothers who did it. Homer and Faye Williams had both done it with their only child Wayne, who was more like a grandchild, they had him so late in life. And they had actually gone bankrupt indulging their doughy, daydreaming boy.

"What if y'all having a hard time findin' the mamas for the same reason you havin' a hard time findin' the boys' bodies?" she said.

At first I thought she meant because they were dead too—as if they died protecting their sons, but then I realized what she meant.

"What if because of the threat—especially at that time—they took their boys and disappeared? I wish to God I had."

It was an interesting theory, one we needed to look into—even though Ada Baker had obviously not vanished with her son. Maybe Cedric was some kind of anomaly. Maybe Ada was the exception that proved Ida's rule. Or maybe Ida was reaching for hope in an essentially hopeless circumstance.

"That's a great thought," I said. "Brilliant, actually."

"I'm gonna see 'bout helpin' Mickey track down the moms," she said. "See if I can't disprove or prove my own theory."

Chapter Thirty-nine

"Just because he had a white kid this time, doesn't mean he didn't abduct black kids when he lived here," Mickey said.

"True," I said, "but it does make it far less likely."

Two days had passed. Frank was still in a coma.

I was discouraged, depressed, and in need of a drink—and drink wasn't far away from where we sat at the old dining table in Second Chances.

"You don't think it could be him?" Mickey said, glancing at me briefly, then away again.

"I'm not ruling it out, but . . ."

"How about this? His mom helps him snatch the kids."

I glanced over at Kenny, who was alternating between coloring and reading comics on the floor not far away.

Camille had taken Wilbur to the doctor. Mickey was babysitting Kenny and the store.

I nodded at Kenny and Mickey lowered his voice.

"Then she also helps him set up the dads and get rid of the bodies," he continued. "Two of them working together like that . . . The bodies could be buried in the woods right out back of here."

I shrugged. "It's possible, but I still think it's unlikely."

The front door opened and Miss Ida and Summer Grantham walked in.

"We came to check on you," Ida said. "Heard what happened. Why you didn't say somethin' the other night on the phone? You okay?"

"Thank you," I said, standing to hug them. "I will be once Frank Morgan wakes up."

They joined us at the table.

Today Summer was rocking an old, faded maroon Madonna T-shirt with jeans and matching Keds. She looked like she would fit in better over coloring with Kenny than sitting with the adults at the dining table.

"What you did," Summer said, "saving that poor boy the way you did . . ."

"That poor boy," Ida said.

"I'm praying for your friend," Summer said.

"Thank you."

We were all quiet a beat.

"Hey Mr. John," Kenny said, "you ever read *Batman: the Dark Knight Returns* by Frank Miller?"

"I haven't, Kenny," I said. "Is it good?"

"It's great. You can borrow when I'm done . . . or we can read it together."

"I'd like that, thank you."

"Speaking of superpowers," Mickey said to Summer, "use yours and tell us if Creepy Gibbons is responsible for what happened to Cedric, Jamal and the others."

She rolled her eyes. "Doesn't work that way. And it's not a superpower."

"Whatta you think?" Ida asked me.

"I think it is a superpower," I said. "She's just being

modest."

"I meant about the boys and Daryl Lee."

"Not ruling anything out, but . . . predators like him usually hunt within their same race and don't usually change their MO."

"But maybe for a short while when he was here," Mickey said, "he didn't have a choice. Maybe what he did here, what they did, was opportunistic, more to do with who was here than his preference."

Something Wayne Williams said to me when I first encountered him at the Omni's arcade six years ago echoed inside me.

Just 'cause I prefer chocolate, don't mean I couldn't go for some vanilla.

Summer nodded, but I couldn't tell if it was to what I had said or Mickey.

"And one more thing," Mickey said, "and this is the biggest of all as far as I'm concerned." He paused for effect, but didn't make eye contact with any of us, which undermined it. "If it was Daryl Lee, it would explain why they stopped," he said. "They stopped here 'cause he moved. They continued somewhere else 'cause that's where he moved to."

I nodded. "You're right," I said. "That is the best argument of all."

"Somebody need to see where all else he lived," Ida said. "See how many missing children there are in those areas."

"I'll talk to Remy Boss about it," I said.

"If it turns out he took any black boys in any of the other places, it would strengthen the case for him doing it here," Summer said.

We nodded our agreement and fell silent for a moment again.

"Has Ada agreed to the tap yet?" Mickey asked Ida.

"No," she said, shaking her head, "and she ain't gonna."

"It's like she doesn't want to know," he said.

"Maybe she doesn't," Ida said, "but not for the reason you think. Once you know, you can't unknow. You can't lie to yourself anymore. No matter how hard you try or how good at it you are."

"Are girls allowed to read Batman too?" Summer asked.

Kenny and I were on the floor in the little toy area. I was reading to him. We both looked up, but I waited for him to answer.

"Sure," he said. "Come on. You can read the girl parts."

She and I smiled at each other at the thought of *girl parts*.

"Is it okay?" she asked me.

"Of course," I said.

She sat down beside us, tucking her feet beneath her legs. As she did, Kenny slid toward me, then eased into my lap.

In that moment, I realized a few things. First, how closed I had been to Kenny, how completely my experience with Martin Fisher had shut me down—and not just Martin but every victim I had encountered—how much loss and pain, death and devastation I had seen. I had been in self-preservation mode—still was, and it had caused me to give far less to Kenny than I otherwise would have. I realized too just how much Kenny was looking for and in need of the attention and affection of a man, a father figure. It was that very vulnerability that most likely led to the capture of many of the victims. Finally, I felt funny with him on

my lap—something I never would have before. After
what I had seen in the original case and then at Daryl Lee
Gibbons's house, I felt awkward having Kenny so close—
not for anything having to do with him or me, but how
it might appear to others in the light of all we had been
dealing with.

"Ooh," Summer said. "This is good."

She slid over next to me, which made me feel better
about how this looked. Before long, Kenny was in her lap,
which made me feel better still.

Chapter Forty

"**Y**ou actually sat across from Wayne Williams," Susan said.

"I did."

I was sitting across from her now—at a table in the back corner of Scarlett's drinking coffee. I found it easier not to drink anything but coffee when I didn't sit at the bar.

Remy Boss had said he would do his best to swing by to talk to me if he could. I was waiting for him and reviewing my notes on the cases—while sipping coffee and talking to Susan.

"How was it?"

"Surreal," I said.

She nodded. "I bet. Did he say anything that made you believe he was . . . innocent? Or guilty or anything?"

"I'm still processing everything he said, so . . . maybe. I'm not sure."

"Look at this," Margaret said from behind the bar. "They say we got snow coming."

She turned up the TV and we all listened.

"Metro Atlanta may see its earliest snowfall on record," a local weather man was saying.

An afternoon regular at the bar said, "Please tell us you're not going to close down, Margaret. Even if it's the storm of the century."

"It's not gonna snow," she said. "It's not, but if it does . . . whole city shuts down. You know that. At the slightest dusting of white powder. Hell, a Martha White Flour truck turned over on 285 and all the commuters stopped and hunkered down in their cars 'cause they thought the white dust was the first sign of flurries."

"Southerners, am I right?" the patron, who had lived here his entire life, said.

"We should have a snow pool," she said. "Bet on whether it's gonna snow or not."

"Yeah," the patron said. "Let's do it. Put me in for twenty for it not to. I don't think it's gonna happen. Or maybe I just don't want it to. Either way . . . puttin' my money where my heart is."

"You believe this?" Susan said, jerking her head back toward the conversation at the bar.

I smiled. "I've never been in snow before," I said.

"Really?"

"Unless I'm blocking out some family trip from childhood."

"It's not gonna snow," she said. "But . . ."

"Yeah?"

"How long you been sober?" Susan asked.

"I've lost track," I said. "A while."

"I thought AA was all about keeping track."

"I'm not a very good member," I said. "And I'm not convinced what Lonnie and those guys do in his little room is actually AA. Why?"

"Just thought . . . if you keep it up . . . and if it does snow—two very big ifs—maybe we can hunker down during the snowstorm together. Rent a couple of movies, eat some pizza. Make out."

"Really? How much sobriety would that require?" I asked. "Just so I know."

Later in the afternoon, right on time, Lonnie came in and Margaret poured him his usual—the shot of bourbon to stare at.

Today, he stared at the drink much longer than he did other days.

Sensing something was wrong, I stood and started walking over toward him.

Instead of sliding the glass back toward Margaret, he lifted it and started to take a drink.

"Wait," I yelled, and rushed over to him.

I grabbed the glass just as it reached his lips, knocking it over, it bouncing down the bar and careening off of it onto the floor behind.

"What're you doin'?" I said.

He shook his head. "I just . . ."

"Come over here with me," I said. "Come on."

I grabbed him by the arm and led him over to my table as Susan wiped down the bar and Margaret cleaned up the glass on the floor behind it.

"Can we get another coffee over here?" I said.

"Sure thing," Susan said. "Coming up."

She had it on the table in front of him by the time we sat down.

"What's going on man?" I said. "Want to go to a meeting?"

He shook his head. "Just can't take it anymore. It's too much. I've held it together so long."

I nodded. "I know you have. You've done great. You really have."

"Losing my business . . . is really gettin' to me. Got

nothing else. No idea what I'm gonna do. Then stirring everything up around Cedric and those others . . . Takes me back to such a bad time. So tired of fighting."

"I know," I said. "I know you are."

"I know you think you do," he said, "but you don't. Think about how long you been doin' it. That's nothing. Hell, I been drinking longer than you been alive. Been sober longer than you've been drinking."

"I didn't mean—"

"I been so strong so long. Been holdin' it all together—for Cedric, for Ada, for my store, for . . . What's the use? Cedric ain't ever comin' back. My store's a lost cause. Ada's got her phone calls, found religion. Don't need me no more. I got nothin'. I'm done fighting. Can't do it no more."

"Drink some of your coffee and let's do a meeting, right here, right now."

"You listening, man? I don't want to do no goddamn meetin'. Don't want to say no goddamn Serenity Prayer. I want a fuckin' drink and keep 'em comin'. Got it?"

"Please," I said. "I need you. I can't do this without you."

"You don't need me, man. You're doin' just fine. Just fine."

"Because of you," I said.

"No," he said. "Not because of me. Because of you. You're doin' it. Not me."

"I couldn't've done it without you," I said. "Can't do it without you. I mean it."

"You don't mean it."

"I do. Don't believe me? Fine. You drink, I drink. You wanna drink? Fuck it, let's drink. Whatta we havin? Susan, give us two bourbons. Make 'em doubles."

She shook her head. "I won't. I can't."

"What kind of bar is this?" I said. "Margaret, come join us. Bring a bottle."

"I would, but I've got to stay behind the bar," she said. "Sorry."

"Fine, we'll move to the bar," I said. "Come on."

As I started to stand, Lonnie grabbed my arm and pulled me back down.

He didn't say anything, just held my arm with one hand and began drinking his coffee with the other.

Later, after Lonnie had gone back to work and I was still waiting for Remy Boss to drop by, Susan walked over to me.

"You weren't bluffing, were you?" she said. "You would have drank with Lonnie, wouldn't you?"

"I wasn't bluffing," I said.

"I didn't think so."

"That mean our snow date is canceled?" I asked.

She frowned. "'Fraid so."

I had almost given up on Remy by the time he finally showed up.

"Only got a minute," he said. "Can't stay."

He didn't even sit down.

"What's up?" he added when I didn't say anything.

"We were wondering if the victims here could be Daryl Lee's and if there were any black victims in the other places where he lived."

"We?"

"Our missing and murdered children group," I said.

"The investigation is just beginning," he said. "It'll

be a while before we know where all he lived and if he even had any other victims. It won't be quick."

"I know, I just—"

"Look, I've tried to be patient with you, but . . . you gotta leave me alone and let me do my job. As a courtesy I'll come and talk to your little group after the investigation is complete, let y'all know anything I can."

His entire attitude had changed. It wasn't that he had been much more than indifferent or slightly patient before, but now he was actually hostile.

"Sorry," I said. "I won't bother you again."

"Lot of people blame you for what happened to Frank Morgan. I'm not one of them. Frank is the professional. You're the . . . whatever you are. Young person. He should have never gone in there, should've never taken you. Whatever happened after that is on him."

I nodded, and thought about it, remembering how I had pressed Frank to go when he did—and to take me with him. Maybe I was to blame.

"This is serious shit," he said. "Fuck up and people get hurt or killed. Just think about that. Now I'm gonna look into these missing kids over here again—like I already told you. And I'm gonna see if there's a Daryl Lee Gibbons connection. I'm gonna do a thorough and professional investigation. I appreciate the information you've given me. Now let me use it."

Chapter Forty-one

I got in my car and I drove.

I drove angrily and aggressively.

It was dark now, traffic had thinned.

I was on 285 driving like I had somewhere to be in a hurry.

I had been at it a while, but my face still stung from embarrassment and frustration. I felt lonely and useless, isolated and guilty.

I wasn't sure how long the blue lights had been flashing before I noticed them, but I bet it had been a while.

I pulled over and put my car in Park, my heart pounding, my eyes bulging.

"Where you headed in such a hurry, son?" the fifty-something gray-headed cop holding the bright light in my face asked.

"Just out for a drive," I said. "Clear my head."

"License and registration. Where do you live?"

I told him as I handed him my documents.

There wasn't much traffic on 285, but what there was streaked by in a windy *whoosh* then disappeared again into the dark night.

"Why do your plates say Florida?"

"I'm a student," I said. "Recently moved up here. "Permanent residence is in Florida."

He studied my license, then pointed his light back in my face. "Why's your name sound so familiar?"

I shrugged. "Not sure. But I get that a lot."

"No, I know. You're the one that . . . They found that dead kid in your apartment."

"Actually, I found him," I said.

"You got that one cop killed. What was his name? And another half-dead, fighting for his life in the hospital right now. I've pulled me over a sure enough by god menace."

I started to explain but knew there was no use.

"Just wait right here," he said, then ambled back to his car.

With Frank in the hospital and no friends on the force, I had no one to call. No friends. Only enemies. Only those who wished me ill.

As alone and isolated as I had felt before, I felt far more so now—alone, isolated, and vulnerable. Very vulnerable.

I sat there, flashing lights illuminating my car and the night around it, and waited.

And waited.

Eventually, another car, this one a dark unmarked, pulled in behind him.

This time two cops approached my vehicle—one on either side.

"Step out of the car," he said.

Stay calm. Don't give them any reason to justify use of force or anything else.

I did as I was told. Slowly. Carefully.

"Hands on the hood," he said. "Spread your legs."

I did, and he patted me down.

As he did, the other cop began searching my car.

"Larry Moore was a good cop," the guy in my car said. "Miss him. The force misses him. The city misses him."

The cop behind me put his mouth to my ear. "Think anyone would miss you?"

I shook my head.

"Hands behind your back," he said.

I did as I was told and he cuffed me.

The cop in the car popped the trunk, walked around, and began searching it.

"Hey Kyle," the cop behind me said, "how many cuffed losers resisting arrest have we had fall into oncoming traffic out here?"

"Not enough, brother. Not enough."

He grabbed my arm and turned me around to face the four lanes of 285 closest to us.

He smelled of cigarettes, fast-food, and aftershave.

"They slow down some when they see our lights," he said, "but not much. Not enough to make a difference. Hell, it'd be better for you if they sped up. Lot better to get eighty-sixed than made a vegetable."

Heart and head racing, I did my best not to let him know how much what he was doing was affecting me.

Hooking his leg around my feet, he began leaning me toward the traffic, my hair blowing in the brisk breeze the cars generated.

"Hey Kyle, could I get you to do me a favor?"

"Anything for a brother, brother."

"Kill our lights."

It took a minute but he did.

Now we were shrouded in darkness, and the speeding cars didn't slow or break until they were on top of us—many of them not even then.

"One little flick of my wrist," he said. "Wonder how many lives I'd save? How many cops?"

"Good cops," Kyle added.

A car was approaching in the lane closest to us, and I could tell he was about to toss me in front of it.

I was going to die without knowing what happened to Cedric Porter or whether or not Wayne Williams was guilty, without knowing or learning or experiencing a million other things that really mattered, and there was nothing I could do about it.

Twenty seconds away.

He adjusted his grip.

Ten.

Repositioned his leg around mine.

Zero.

He dropped me.

I began to flail but with my hands cuffed behind me there wasn't much I could do. Nothing to grab. Nothing to grab with.

Falling.

Reaching.

Grasping.

Then he grabbed me again and pulled me back.

Tossing me back in my car, he uncuffed me, dropped a ticket for the largest amount allowed by law on top of me, and walked with Kyle to their cars without saying another word.

Turning their lights back on to make a hole in the oncoming traffic, they sped off into the dark night.

I sat there for a long time.

How had this become my life?

I had never felt so helpless, so small, so defenseless.

Eventually I had my breathing back under control. I

cranked the car and turned on the lights.

Taking the next exit, I found the nearest payphone and called Harry Bosch.

I hadn't spoken to him in years, but he had said to call him whenever I needed to, and with Frank in a coma and my dad not speaking to me, I couldn't think of anyone better to call than Bosch.

Such was my trust for Bosch that even after all this time I felt comfortable to call him collect—the only option available to me at the moment.

As I dialed, pulse pounding in my throat, I searched the dark side street for patrol cars—far more afraid of them than any other nocturnal urban threats.

At my request, the operator let it ring a long time, but there was no answer.

"Is there another number you'd like me to try, sir?" she asked.

"No ma'am, thank you," I said. "I don't have anyone else to call."

I climbed back into my car and cranked it.

Breathe. Calm down. Frank's not available. Neither is Harry. That's okay. You have what you need. Find your center. Grow up. You're not a kid anymore. Here's your chance to prove it.

I pulled up the on-ramp and back onto 285.

I had never driven the entire perimeter at one time before. I was going to tonight. I was going to obey the speed limit and drive far more cautiously than I had before, but I was not going to be deterred.

I did it without getting stopped again. Sixty-four miles in a little less than an hour.

Stopping at a Circle K store when I had finished circling the city, literally driving around in a circle because I didn't know what else to do, I refueled and took off again—this time down 20 toward Grady to check on Frank.

The city was different at night. It had an ethereal quality, as if it wasn't the same place it was during the day, as if the night city and the day city weren't the same city at all.

Frank was still in a coma, still in ICU, so I did the only thing I could do—I sat alone in the empty ICU waiting room and waited.

I waited because I didn't know what else to do. What I was waiting for or how long I would wait for it wasn't something I was clear about.

After a while of just waiting, I decided there was something else I could do.

Locating the small, empty chapel, I went in and prayed. I prayed for Frank, for his full recovery and no lasting damage at all. I prayed for Lonnie and the demon he was battling. I prayed for Summer and the different but equally difficult demon she was battling.

I prayed for a while, then went back up to ICU waiting, where eventually I fell fast asleep.

When I woke the next morning, families of very sick patients were beginning to fill the room, preparing for the first of four short visits they were granted each day.

Easing up out of my chair, I made my way into the hallway and was about to leave when I saw Frank's wife, Evelyn, and daughter walking up.

Haggard and sad, the thin, pale skin of their faces looked like parchment stretched too tightly across the bones beneath.

"John?" Evelyn said. "What're you doing here?"

"Hey, John," Becca said with a little wave. She was Frank's thirteen-year-old daughter, and seeing her made me wonder where his twelve-year-old son was.

"Just came down to be close to him, to stay with him

and pray for him last night."

"You stayed all night? That means a lot. Thank you."

"Wish I could do more."

"Becca, would you go down to that coffee machine and get me a cup?" Evelyn asked, handing her daughter a dollar.

"Can I get one too?"

"Sure honey," she said, handing her another dollar. "Help yourself."

When Becca was gone, Evelyn turned back to me. "They say if he doesn't wake up in the next day or so, chances are he won't. Please pray even more, John. I don't want to lose him. I can't. I need to have the big ol' square thing around. And the kids . . . how would they ever . . .""

Fighting back tears, she patted me on the arm and pushed past me.

"Come on Becca," she called, "it's almost time for visitation."

"Thought you wanted coffee?"

"After. Let's put on our best, bright faces for daddy."

As I was leaving, I ran into Don Paulk, who was arriving.

He was here to pray with one of his parishioners prior to her surgery.

A founder of the church, along with his brother Earl and their wives, Don had been particularly good to me since I moved to Atlanta—especially at the end of the LaMarcus Williams case when everything went so badly. LaDonna, who I had class with, was his daughter.

"I was planning on coming down to the college to talk to you today," he said.

He's heard about the lawsuit.

"Your professors are concerned about how many

classes you're missing," he added. "How are you, John?"

I shrugged. "I'm okay, I guess."

"Can I take you to lunch after your classes today so we can really talk?"

I hesitated a moment.

"You are planning to attend your classes today, aren't you?"

The truth was I wasn't.

"That's one of the things they wanted me to talk to you about," he said. "You can't miss any more and pass."

"Maybe I should just drop them for this quarter and start again next one," I said.

"I'd hate to see you do that," he said. "It would mess up your schedule and when you can graduate—and many people who drop out don't ever seem to start back. Tell you what, go today, then let's go to lunch together and see if we can't figure it out, okay?"

"Remember the little boy who was found dead in my room?" I said.

He nodded.

"His mother's threatening to bring a lawsuit against me," I said.

"I'm so sorry to hear that. Are you—"

"She plans to name the college and the church since the apartment was being used for a dorm."

He didn't seem surprised.

"We can talk about that today too," he said.

"But—"

"We can figure everything out, John. I promise."

Chapter Forty-two

I had every intention of attending class and going to lunch with Pastor Don.

Then Mickey called.

"Found Jaquez Anderson's dad," he said. "'Bout to go talk to him. Wanna go?"

I didn't answer right away.

"Come on," he said. "I've got a feeling we're gonna solve this thing. I really do. I've been working hard on it, but I could use your help. You know I don't like doing interviews."

"How can a reporter not like doing interviews?" I said.

"I always worked with a partner. I did the writing. He did the research and reporting and chasing down of stories. I can do it. I just don't like to."

"You pickin' me up?" I said.

"Ten minutes away."

While waiting for Mickey to arrive, I reviewed my notes on the case.

Cedric Porter, Jamal Jackson, Quentin Washington, Jaquez Anderson, Duke Ellis, and Vaughn Smith. All missing. All between the ages of ten and fourteen. All vanished during the height of the Atlanta Child Murders.

All living with single mothers who were neglectful. All
of them lived off this end of Memorial Drive—all but
Vaughn Smith that was. He had lived up off Wesley Chapel.
Cedric and Jamal had both lived here in Memorial Manor.
Quentin Washington and Jaquez Anderson had lived in an
apartment complex on the other side of Memorial, Duke
Ellis in a house down off North Hairston.

So far every dad we had interviewed except for
Cedric's had articles of his son's clothing or other items
planted in his home or vehicle and had been suspected by
the authorities of having taken his son.

The only parents we had yet to track down were
those of Jaquez Anderson and Vaughn Smith.

I was glad Mickey had found Jaquez's dad, but
believed finding Vaughn's was more important since he
lived outside the pattern area.

In fact, it was one of three big questions about this
case. Why does Vaughn's location break the pattern? Why
does Cedric, Sr. not having items planted break the pattern?
Where are the boys or their bodies?

And then it hit me.

According to Cedric, Sr., he wasn't Cedric, Jr.'s real
father. Was that true? Did the killer know? Was that why he
didn't have any clothing or other items planted in his home
or vehicle? If so, that would explain why—and it might
help us identify the killer. I'd have to look into that some
more.

Major Anderson worked at the Richway store on
Covington Highway.

Richway was a discount department store owned and
operated by Rich's. It was known for, among other things,

the colorful raised wedge skylights on the roof. Its logo was an orange sunrise with black block letters beneath it, representing, the store carried everything under the sun.

We met Major on a loading dock in the back of the store during his brief morning break.

The day was cold and clear, a bright but impotent sun high in the sky.

"Whatch y'all think?" he said. "It gonna snow?"

He had big, bright eyes and a bushy beard that looked shiny in the morning light. Young, thick, and muscular, he still wore a back brace designed for lifting and I wondered if it was company policy.

"I hope so," I said.

"Not gonna happen," Mickey said.

The plum-colored smudges beneath Mickey's small eyes and his pale, drawn skin evidenced his exhaustion. Which when added to his scraggly, untrimmed reddish beard and longish, unkempt strawberry-blond hair made him look a little maniacal, and I could tell the case was getting to him far more than he had let on.

"I don't know," he said, "I'm kinda thinkin' it will."

"We shall soon see," Mickey said.

"So, y'all want to talk to me about Jaquez? I pray for that little man every day."

He held his work gloves down by his side, bringing them up occasionally when using his hands to talk, the worn-smooth fingers flapping in the breeze as he did.

"We do," I said. "Is that okay?"

"Every day," he repeated. "Without fail. I don't mind talkin' to you, but I don't know anything."

"Any idea where he might be or what might have happened to him?" I said.

He shook his head. "No idea. First thought I had was his mama got herself into some trouble and the boy paid the price, like maybe she owed somebody somethin' for some drugs and they took him just to get her to pay up, but . . . after just a few minutes with her I knew that wasn't the case. So I ain't gonna be no help."

"Did the police look at you?"

"Sure. Good and hard for a few minutes, but I didn't have nothin' to do with it, and they moved on."

"Did Jaquez ever mention a man in the area who the kids called Creepy?"

He shook his head. "That who took my boy?"

"We honestly don't know," I said. "Just trying to find out."

"I wish I knew somethin' that would help," he said. "I'd do anything to get my boy back, but . . . his moms and I wasn't together so I . . . . just don't know anything."

"Do you recall if some of Jaquez's clothes or toys were planted in your house or car during that time?"

His eyes grew wide and he stopped moving for a moment. "Those were his? Never could figure out where those came from or how they got in my place. Why were they—who put them there?"

"That's what we're trying to find out," I said.

"I don't get it. What would that . . ."

"Maybe try to make the cops think you had him," I said.

"Oh."

We were quiet a moment as he thought about it.

"How'd you even know to ask?" he said.

"It happened in some other cases of missing children," I said. "Our theory is someone planted them to put suspicion on the fathers."

"What other cases?"

I told him.

"Any of those names sound familiar?"

He nodded. "Vaughn."

"Vaughn Smith?" I said, my pulse rising.

"Yeah."

"He lived up off Wesley Chapel," I said. "How'd you know him?"

"He get taken too?" he asked.

I nodded.

"Oh my God. Was it Wayne Williams?"

"We don't think so," I said. "We really don't. How'd you know Vaughn?"

"Used to take Jaquez out for the day sometimes," he said. "Grab a burger, go for a walk, climb Stone Mountain, go to the mall, shit like that. Sometimes we'd go to a movie right there on Memorial Drive not far from where he lived with his mother. Cordelia Smith worked at the theater. Vaughn, her kid, was always with her. Single mom. No help with him. He'd hang out, watch movies all day. We got to know them. He'd sit with us sometimes."

I nodded.

He looked at the plastic watch strapped to his left wrist.

"I gotta get back to work," he said. "Let me know if you find out anything, will you?"

"We will," I said, and he rushed back inside the building.

"So," I said, "Vaughn Smith lived outside of our geographic pattern, but his mom worked right in the middle of it, and brought him to work with her—a lot from the sounds of it."

"Now the only anomaly on our list is Cedric's dad not having any clothes planted in his place or car," Mickey said.

"Maybe he did," I said.

"He told us he didn't."

"What he told us was that he wasn't Cedric's dad," I said.

"Oh shit, that's right."

We were quiet a moment, thinking about it.

"Whatta we do now?" Mickey said.

"Would still like to talk to the other mothers."

"Can't believe they're so hard to find," he said.

"Unless Ida's theory is right—is she still helping you look?" He nodded. "It's pretty simple really," I said. "Their names have changed—or were never the same as those of their sons to begin with. They're poor so move around more. Different name in a different location—hell, that's what people trying not to be found do."

"Oh my God this is gonna make such a good story," he said. "If this doesn't wind up being connected to the original case, I've got two books—one on the Atlanta Child Murders and one on this one."

That reminded me of what Frank had said about Mickey and his motives, and made me want to get away from him.

"I'm gonna keep looking for the mothers and I've got a couple of other things to check out," he said. "Can I drop you somewhere? Don't you have class today?"

Chapter Forty-three

Regretting not going to class or lunch with Pastor Don, feeling like a self-sabotaging loser, worried about and experiencing guilt over Frank, I threw myself into my work.

Quietly, because my roommate was asleep on the other side of the thin wall, I dove into the trace evidence in the Atlanta Child Murders case like never before.

With my phone off the hook, I sat in the middle of my floor surrounded by massive amounts of data.

Most violent crimes involve physical contact between perpetrators and their victims. When this occurs, there is often an inadvertent transfer of microscopic debris—a person-to-person cross transfer. This transfer constitutes evidence and most often consists of hairs and fibers. This transfer of hairs and fibers, their discovery, collection, examination, and identification as trace evidence can be critical in linking a suspect to a victim or a crime scene.

This was certainly true of the Atlanta Child Murders case.

Textile fibers can be exchanged between two individuals, between an individual and an object, and between two objects. When fibers are matched with a specific source—a fabric from the victim, suspect, or crime scene—a value is placed on the association. This value is dependent on the type of fibers found, their color, variation of color, the quantity found, the location of fibers at the crime scene or on the victim, and the number of different fibers at the crime scene or on the victim that match the clothing of the suspect.

Whether a fiber is transferred and detected is dependent on the nature and duration of contact between the suspect and the victim or crime scene, the persistence of fibers after the transfer, and the type of fabric involved in contact.

A fiber is the smallest unit of a textile material that has a length many times greater than its diameter. Fibers can occur naturally as plant and animal fibers, but they can also be manufactured.

When two people come in contact or when contact occurs with an item from the crime scene, there's a possibility that fiber transfer will take place. The transfer is not automatic and will not always take place. Some fibers don't shed or don't shed much. A big factor in the transfer of trace evidence is the length of time between the actual physical contact and the collection of clothing items from the suspect or victim. If the victim remains immobile, very little fiber loss will occur, whereas the suspect's clothing will often lose transferred fibers quickly. The longer the passage of time between the crime and the processing of the suspect, the greater the likelihood of finding transferred fibers on the clothing of the suspect decreases.

Fibers are gathered at a crime scene with tweezers, tape, or a vacuum. Typically, they come from clothing, drapery, wigs, carpeting, furniture, and blankets. They are first determined to be natural, manufactured, or a mix of both. Natural fibers come from plants and animals. Synthetic fibers such as rayon, acetate, and polyester are made from long chains of molecules called polymers. Determining the shape and color of fibers from any of these fabrics is done by examining them beneath a microscopic.

In the Atlanta Child Murders case the only clue being found with any consistency, a clue that would only be valuable if a suspect was uncovered, was the presence of trace evidence on several of the bodies and their clothing.

The fibers were sent to the Georgia State Crime Lab for analysis, where Larry Peterson was able to isolate two distinct types—a violet-colored acetate fiber and a coarse yellow-green nylon fiber with a distinctive trilobed quality found in few carpets.

When the discovery of the fibers began to be reported in the newspaper, the killer began stripping the bodies and throwing them into the river, most likely in an attempt to wash away the trace evidence.

Once he became a suspect, Wayne Williams's home and car were searched and provided numerous fibers and human and canine hairs similar to those authorities had been collecting from the victims' bodies—beginning with a tuft of carpet fibers in the tennis shoe of Eric Middlebrooks. The floors of the home where Williams lived with his parents were covered with yellow-green carpeting, and he had a dog. When comparisons from the samples removed from the victims were compared to those of the Williamses' home, they showed good consistency.

FBI experts analyzed samples from the Williamses' rugs with special equipment and the help of DuPont, and were able to ascertain that the fibers came from a Boston-based textile company. The fiber, which is known as Wellman 181B, had been sold to numerous carpet companies, each of which used its own dye. This led to the discovery that the most likely source was the West Point

Pepperell Corporation in Georgia. The company's Luxaire English Olive color matched that found in the Williamses' home.

The company had only made that type of carpet for about one year, distributing about sixteen thousand yards of it throughout the South—a very small amount adding up to about only eighty homes in Georgia or 1 in 7792 homes in Atlanta.

With the help of Chevrolet, investigators determined that there was a 1 in 3,828 chance that a victim acquired the fiber from a random contact with a car that had this carpeting installed.

Then both the odds from the home and the car were calculated—a figure that came to nearly 1 in 30,000,000.

Of course, Williams's defense team attempted to discredit the fiber evidence with the argument that a particular fiber might be in the home or vehicle of any number of people.

But when I considered the probability of a person having a particular carpet with a very unique type of fiber, the same person a particular bedspread with a particular set of light green cotton fibers blended with violet acetate fibers, and that same person also driving a 1970 Chevrolet station wagon and owning a dog who shed the type of hairs found on the victims, the evidence was overwhelming.

When I read that Larry Peterson's fiber analysis work in the case had been reviewed favorably by the world-famous microanalyst Walter McCrone—someone I was familiar with because of his work on the Shroud of Turin—I was even more convinced.

Another expert called in to consult on the fiber evidence had a connection to me, Florida, my dad, and even Susan's dad. Lynn Henson, a quiet young woman and an expert on fibers and threats who worked in the Florida

State Crime lab in Tallahassee, had been called in to analyze the evidence and help provide a decisive evaluation.

Henson—whose testimony the year before figured prominently in the Florida trial of Ted Bundy that both Dad and Susan's dad, Tom Daniels, had worked on—testified in Williams's trial that synthetic fibers found on one of the victim's bodies showed no significant differences from the samples taken from Williams's home and station wagon.

Suddenly, I was homesick for Florida—for my town, my family and friends, for Anna and Merrill, and a million other things I couldn't even name.

I was overwhelmed with the urge to pack up everything, jump in the car, and head home.

Maybe I should.

I had promised Frank I'd go home next week for Thanksgiving, and though until this moment I hadn't really planned on going, what if I went home and didn't come back?

The longing for home, for any kind of comfort I could find there pulled me like never before in my entire life. But I wasn't running, wasn't hiding, wasn't going home until I had done everything I could do for both cases I was working on. I couldn't.

I couldn't leave, but what I could do was call home. I could at least do that.

But the moment I placed the receiver back on the cradle to make the call, my phone began ringing.

Snatching it up before it could wake Rick, I whispered my hello into it.

"Who the hell you been on the phone with?" Margaret asked.

"No one. What's wrong?"

"Camille's little boy Kenny," she said. "He's missing."

Chapter Forty-four

A single squad car was outside Second Chances. It was the only indication at all that anything was going on.

Margaret, Susan, Rand, and Lonnie were standing at the corner of the building near Scarlett's when I ran up.

"He never made it to his mama's shop from the bus stop," Susan said.

"Is anyone in there with her?" I asked.

"Her other boy," Lonnie said. "She ain't about to let him out of her sight."

My heart sank even more as I smelled the alcohol on Lonnie's breath.

"Is this related to Cedric and the other boys from a few years back?" Margaret asked.

"It's gotta be, doesn't it?" Lonnie said. "But . . . why wait so long in between? Why now? What does it mean for Cedric? Why would he—"

"I'm gonna go see if I can help," I said.

"Want me to go with you?" Lonnie asked.

"Are you okay to?" I asked.

His eyes locked on to mine and he nodded.

"Sure then. Thanks."

My legs felt weak as we walked the two short store fronts to her shop.

"You okay?" Lonnie asked.

I shook my head.

"Me either."

"When'd you start drinkin' again?"

"Little while back," he said. "Been hidin' it. Couldn't today."

The little bell jingled as we walked in the door, and Camille looked up, her red, impossibly tired eyes moist, her thin, light skin drawn.

"Get him the fuck out of here," she said when she saw me. "Get the fuck out of here. This is your fault. You did this. Stirring all this up again, making my little boy a mark. Get him out of here now."

"Come on," Lonnie said, grabbing me by the arm and helping me as my knees began to buckle. "Let's go. She's just upset."

He got me turned around and headed out the door.

"We're out here if you need us," he said over his shoulder.

"Find Mickey," she said. "Get Mickey here now."

"Okay," he said. "You got it. Anything else, we're right outside."

When Margaret and Susan saw Lonnie helping me, they ran to meet us.

"What's wrong?" Margaret said. "What happened?"

"Are you okay?" Susan asked.

"He'll be fine," Lonnie said. "Camille's just upset. Looking for someone to blame."

"She's blaming *you*?" Susan said.

"Come on," Margaret said. "Come in here and sit down."

Margaret held the door and Lonnie and Susan helped me in.

"I'm okay," I said. "I can walk. I was just . . . I'm okay. Can I use your phone?"

"Sure, honey," Margaret said. "Help yourself."

I walked over on steadier legs, picked up the phone and paged Mickey.

While I waited for him to call back, Susan brought me a cup of coffee.

"Thanks."

"What's going on, John?" she said.

"I don't know."

"You've got to," she said. "You know more about all of this than everyone else put together. Why now? Why so long after Cedric and the others were taken?"

"I don't know," I said. "I wish I did."

"I bet you do," she said. "If you just let yourself think about everything. I bet you know."

"I don't."

"You have to," she said. "We've got a little boy missing and a snowstorm on the way."

Thankfully, the phone rang.

I snatched it up.

It wasn't Mickey, but a supplier looking for Margaret. I quickly got a number and told him she'd call him back later.

All around us the bar was chaos and confusion. Everyone was talking over each other in emotion-strained voices.

"There are too many interruptions here," Susan said. "Too much noise. Go back to your apartment and work on it there. I'll talk to Mickey when he calls. I'll have him call you at your place."

"I need to call Remy Boss too."

"Are you kidding? I heard the way that prick spoke to you yesterday. He's not gonna do shit. You know that."

"Bobby Battle then," I said. "Since I can't call Frank. Some detective needs to know. This can't be handled like just another missing kid case."

"So call him," she said. "From your place."

I nodded. "Okay," I said. "I'm not sure I can come up with anything, but I know I can't here. Thank you."

As I turned to leave, I saw something I had hoped never to.

With Margaret's attention at the door and our attention on the phone and each other, Lonnie had reached behind the bar, removed a bottle of bourbon, and was pouring himself drinks and knocking them back as quickly as he could.

"Lonnie, no," I said.

"Can't take it no more," he said. "It's all too much. All of it. I'll stop drinking when they find that little boy, then I'll figure out what to do with the rest of my life, but for now I'm gonna drink."

Chapter Forty-five

I didn't know what Susan expected from me, but I was pretty sure I wouldn't be able to do it.

I was an alcoholic college dropout who had gotten the best friend I had in Atlanta shot and maybe killed. I was barely an adult—some would say I wasn't yet. What could I do?

I could try.

I could go over everything again, add in everything new, including little Kenny's disappearance, and see if anything made any better sense.

Where was Mickey? Why hadn't he called back yet?

As I was pulling everything off my second wall to reexamine and repost, my phone rang.

It was Susan.

"Still no word from Mickey," she said. "Cop took Camille's statement and has just left. We've convinced Lonnie to switch over to coffee, but he was able to pour a lot down in him before we did. We're all closing early out of respect—but we would've had to anyway. Snow's coming sooner than expected. News is telling everyone to get supplies and get inside and stay there. Get back to work. I'll keep you updated and have Mickey call you the moment I hear from him."

As soon as we hung up, I called Bobby Battle.

"Figured I'd be hearin' from you," he said.

"You heard?"

"Yeah, and we're doubling up our efforts. Because of the snowstorm," he said. "Not because we believe there's a serial killer at work. There's not. Understand? There is no serial killer. Frank didn't think so either. I gotta get back to work."

The line went dead.

I hung up and returned to my wall.

Six black boys. All missing. All largely unsupervised, unparented. All with a connection to this area. Now over four years later, and after we start looking into it, another one. What does it mean? Is it even related? How can it not be? It might not be.

Absentee fathers set up for the abductions. No bodies. No evidence. Ada Baker getting calls from Cedric. No reports of any other mothers receiving calls. What does it mean? Cedric's dad not having items planted. What does it mean? Maybe Cedric's case is the anomaly, different from all the rest, the exception that proves the rule, the variation that points to the pattern. If so, what does it mean?

Why was Cedric running back toward the apartment complex? Who or what was he running from? What or who was he running to? What was his mom really doing during that time?

Did Daryl Lee Gibbons kill Cedric and or the other boys and bury them in the woods? If he did, why was Kenny taken and who had taken him?

Where were the bodies?

I stepped over to my little bookshelves in the corner and withdrew a forensic book and looked up methods of disposing of bodies, as I thought of what Wayne Williams said about how John Wayne Gacy did it.

My phone rang and I jumped.

Small voice. Crying. Distraught. Difficult to understand.

It was Frank's daughter, Becca.

"John . . . my daddy's not waking up. He won't wake up. Oh, John, I don't want my daddy to die. Please pray for him. Please help. Please don't let God take my daddy."

"I will," I said. "I will right now."

As soon as we hung up, I dropped to the floor and began to intercede for Frank. Sincerely, fervently, without self-consciousness and with no regard for dignity or decorum.

"Please heal Frank and return him to his little girl," I pleaded. "Please help me find Kenny and return him to his mom. Please."

Then something about the disposal of bodies resurfaced in my mind. What was it?

The phone rang again.

"He had no idea," Susan said. "He'll be callin' you in a minute. We're closing down here in about a half hour. You need me for anything?"

"I'll call you if I do."

"It better be in the next thirty minutes. Once I get home I won't be able to get out again. I'll be stranded. Everyone will. Whatever you do, do it fast."

"You sure there's nothing else you can tell me about Cedric's disappearance?"

"Like what?"

"Where was he running? Who to? Who from?"

"I don't know. I've told you."

"I need to go," I said. "Don't want to miss Mickey's call."

Mickey called a couple of minutes later.

"John, what the hell's goin' on, man?"

"Where are you?" I said.

"Don't be mad. I've been following up on some leads. Not far from where Daryl Lee was," he said. "I've got to get on the road to make it back before the storm hits, but I wanted to tell you a couple of things."

"Okay."

"You're not gonna like them."

"Tell me anyway and quick."

"Did you know Summer Grantham's been involved in cases like this before? She sort of specializes in missing kids. She's been a suspect in a couple of them. She's not right, man. She has what she claims is a daughter, but she's a runaway—or so they claim. I'm not so sure Grantham didn't take her. Anyway, she's not her biological daughter. Grantham's been quoted in some old newspaper articles I found as saying God put her here on earth to save at-risk kids. I think that's what she thinks she's doing, man. And get this—when Cedric and the other boys disappeared, she lived in Memorial Manor."

"Why're you down close to Stockbridge?" I said.

"On my way back from McDonough. Been tryin' to find her place. Wanted to be sure before I told you. I think she has Cedric. Maybe the others too. I don't know. But him for sure."

"What makes you think that?" I said.

"The other thing you're not gonna like," he said. "I've got a deep undercover journalist buddy of mine. He's hardcore. Nothing he won't or can't do. He specializes in deep background so he doesn't have to be concerned about whether something's legal or not. Doesn't matter. Understand?"

"Get to the point, Mickey, we're running out of time here."

"I had him bug Ada Baker's phone when she refused to let the police do it."

"You did what?"

"Yeah. The calls are real man. They're coming from a kid who sounds like he could be Cedric. The call came from McDonough—where Summer lives. No one was home. Do you think it was because she was there taking Kenny? Should I go back? Kenny, man. What a sweet fuckin' kid. I mean, fuck."

And then it hit me.

"Summer doesn't have him," I said. "But I think I know who does."

Chapter Forty-six

"The night Cedric disappeared," I said, "he came here."

"Snow already comin' down," Annie Mae Dozier said, looking past me into the night. "Won't be long 'til everything grind to a halt."

She had just opened her door to my incessant knocking, and was now watching the snow through blinking eyes and big glasses.

Snow was flurrying and falling, the world outside undergoing a sea change.

I took a step into her apartment and she had no choice but to back in.

I closed the door behind me.

"This is where he came when he was upset," I said. "This is where he was running to that night."

"Sure wouldn't be to his sorry no-good mama," she said.

"But he still calls her," I said. "After all this time, he still calls her. Why is that?"

She shrugged her bony shoulders and gave me an expression like she wouldn't care to hazard a guess.

"He calls her from McDonough," I said. "Where your daughter the pharmacist who makes good money but can't have kids lives. Where you yourself will soon be living."

She didn't say anything.

Her small head looked shrunken atop her slumping shoulders, her eyes even more hooded behind her big glasses.

"He was upset and he came here."

"'Cause his mama was out turnin' a trick for one of the mens who'd touched little Cedric—right out in them there woods like animals. It a wonder Cedric didn't see them as he ran by."

"He's upset—maybe even more than usual, but more, less, the same, you've had enough. No more. Your daughter can take him. She can be a good mama to him, and you a good grandma."

"Nobody else linin' up to do it," she said. "Tell you that."

"You kidnapped a child," I said.

She shook her head. "No. He wanted to go. Wanted to be away from all the . . . said would it be all right if he call her sometime. But that all he want with her, just to let her know he okay."

"You stayed behind to make sure no one suspected you, but you needn't have bothered. Cops didn't do much lookin' at all."

"I gots to sit down," she said.

She eased her way over to the sofa and bent a little ways but seemed to be stuck. I stepped over and helped her down.

She was even thinner and bonier than I realized, and couldn't have weighed more than ninety pounds.

"Much 'bliged," she said.

I sat down across from her.

"Why'd you stay so long?"

"I stay with them lots. Not here much. Just enough. Her old place was small. Wasn't sure I wanted to move. I got to see him plenty. Still get to be here close to my friends, my gentlemen callers."

I smiled. I wanted to do more. Merely smiling showed enormous restraint.

"Did y'all take all the boys or just Cedric?"

"What all boys?" she said.

"Did Laney Mitchell come over here that night?"

"Who?"

"Laney Mitchell, co-owner of Scarlett's, the little bar on the other side of—"

"Oh, her. No. Why?"

"She ran after Cedric when she saw him running back here."

"Nobody but him. I looked all around. Made sure he wasn't followed."

"Why're you being so forthcoming?" I asked. "Not that I don't appreciate it, but I am surprised."

"Your questions were different," she said. "And the stuff those other womens was sayin' you said about . . . all that other . . . Knew it just a matter of time 'til you be comin' back."

I waited but she didn't say anything else.

"And?"

"And what? Oh. You can't prove anything, can't prove I did anything."

I was puzzled.

"Mickey Davis, a reporter who's helping me, is in McDonough right now waiting for me to call with your daughter's address. You can give it to me and he can go get Cedric, or I can call the police and they can go."

"Go where?" she said.

"I just told you."

"And I tol' you we seen you comin', boy. They long gone—gone and you nor nobody else ain't never gonna find 'em."

"She ran with him?" I said. "Mind giving me the address so Mickey can check it out?"

"Help yo-self," she said, and gave me the address.

"May I borrow your phone?"

"Be my guest, but you shouldn't have that poor boy traipsing around down there on a fool's errand when it about to snow."

"**S**hit, John, I thought I was coming down here to find Cedric and Kenny and the others, and instead I got nothin' and now I'm stranded down here. I need to be with Camille, need to be helpin' find Kenny and I'm . . . fuckin' stuck down here."

"No one's there?"

"No."

"Is it an empty house?"

"No, it's a fully furnished home. Got pictures of Ms. Dozier and a woman I'm guessing is her daughter, but no boys. And there's a note addressed to you on the table."

"You're kidding."

"Can't make shit like this up."

"Do you mind reading it?"

"Got shit else to do, do I?"

He opened the letter and began to read.

"Dear Mr. Jordan. If you're reading this it means Mom was right. She's a wily old goat. I'll give her that. We have vanished and will be extremely difficult if not impossible to find. But I'm asking you not to look. Not to report us to the authorities and not to look yourself. I'm asking this not for me or my mother, but for Cedric. He's been through so much. Abuse like you can't imagine. He's just now beginning to trust and heal and begin to see what he might be able to be. Don't take that away from him. Please. Think of the pitiful little child, consider the young man he's becoming. Please pray about it and do the right thing."

That was it. A completely unexpected thing.

"So," Mickey said, "she only has Cedric. Where is Kenny? Who has Kenny?"

"I don't know."

"I'm stranded way the fuck down here," he said. "You've got to find him. Please."

We ended the call and I looked at Annie Mae Dozier again, this time with a new and greater appreciation.

"That was impressive," I said.

"We been protectin' that boy for some time now. Learned a thing or two 'bout it."

"They've gone without you," I said.

She shrugged her bony shoulders again, and this time scrunched her face up in a way that seemed to multiply the dark freckles on her face.

"Too old and slow to run."

"You're giving him up—him and your daughter," I said.

"'Greater love hath no man known than to lay down his life for another,'" she said.

I had always thought of that Bible verse in terms of dying for someone, but she was right. Laying down her life—what was left of it anyway—was exactly what she was doing, and it was astounding.

"And you didn't take the other boys?" I said. "Don't know what happened to them?"

"Know nothin' 'bout no other boys."

"Last question," I said, "and I'll leave you alone. What was Cedric running from? What was he so upset about?"

"Didn't say. Never has said. I got no idea. Maybe he did see his moms out in the woods rutting like an animal. I just know it was bad. Final straw for him and us."

Chapter Forty-seven

I walked back to my apartment in the falling snow, humbled, perhaps even a little humiliated.

The night air was thin and cold and easy to breathe, the swirling white snow magical somehow.

Was Kenny, lifeless or otherwise, out in it?

Where was he? Who had him?

It was all that mattered right now, and I couldn't figure it out.

When I entered my apartment I found a note from Rick saying he had gone to spend his snow day at his girlfriend's place.

In my room, I ripped everything off my second wall, scattered it on the floor, and sat in the middle of it.

Rather than focusing narrowly, I intentionally kept my mind broad and open, flittering randomly from thing to thing like a butterfly drunk on spring.

This time, don't just think about the cases. Think about everything you've encountered since stepping into this little community.

As I continued to think, continued to feel the pressure of the clock pounding its time in my head, my mind sped up.

My butterfly became a bee and I buzzed around from item to item trying to mentally cross-pollinate seemingly disparate bits of information to see what they might produce.

Nothing came of it.

It was all too much.

Kenny was going to die and I couldn't stop it.

He's dead already. So's Frank.

I could feel myself beginning to panic, and I wanted a drink in the worst kind of way.

Stop. Stop it. Breathe. Work yourself up into a frenzy, and you won't be any good to Kenny or anyone else.

I'm no good now.

I took a deep breath and then another and another.

"God grant me the serenity to accept the things I cannot change, the courage to change the—"

My mind hit on something, some connection, then it was gone—too quick for me to grasp.

What was it?

It was no good. I couldn't get it back.

Get out of your head, back into the moment. Start over.

"God grant me the serenity to accept the things I cannot change, the courage to change the things I can, and the wisdom to know the difference."

You can't change the circumstances. Stop trying. You can't control the world. Let go.

"God grant me the serenity to accept the things I cannot change, the courage to change the things I can, and the wisdom to know the difference."

What can you do? You can breathe. You can think. You can do what you can. Nothing more. Nothing else. And it's enough.

"God grant me the serenity to accept the things I cannot change, the courage to change the things I can, and the wisdom to know the difference."

Cedric was the anomaly. He was different. Why?

Think about everything. Take it all in. Let go of preconceived notions of what things mean. See them for only what they are. Remove contexts. Remove juxtapositions.

I thought again about where the bodies could be, then back to what Wayne Williams had said about John Wayne Gacy.

And then I had it.

I didn't like it, but I had it. Or thought I did.

I rushed outside.

Raised in Florida, I didn't have a winter wardrobe, and what I had on now—a button-down over a T-shirt—was inadequate in the extreme. I didn't care.

I ran toward the woods. Just like Cedric had.

Blanketed in white, the silent city was serene.

I thought about how I just used the Serenity Prayer to calm myself, as a kind of self-talk that would help me deal with the bad patterns in my thinking. I had done the same thing at the hospital while experiencing the guilt over Frank.

The wooded area separating Memorial Manor from the shops on Memorial Drive looked like an isolated mountain forest, each limb and leaf snow-dusted and picturesque.

Continuing past the woods, I ran up behind the shops and around the corner of Scarlett's to the front.

Eerie. Abandoned. Everything closed. No traffic on Memorial.

It was as if I were the sole survivor of a cold, harsh apocalyptic nuclear winter.

The pinkish-orange lighted letters of Peachtree Pizza's sign shone brightly in the hazy night. I thought about the guy who now called himself Rand Nola and what he said he saw the night Cedric vanished.

Had the other little boys been among his customers?

Did they collect cans, scrape up their money to buy a pie together? Did they come here for pizza while their mothers drank at Scarlett's the way Cedric's had? Had Vaughn Smith's busy working mom stopped here for pizza on her way home? She probably let him rent a video too—something Lonnie would have a record of.

I had to get in to check. But how?

I walked over and pulled on the door, trying to figure some way to break in without breaking the glass and letting snow in.

The door rattled but didn't give.

"Whatta you doin'?" Rand Nola asked.

He had just come out of his pizza place and was locking the door.

Think fast.

"You saw how Lonnie was drinking earlier," I said.

"Yeah?"

"Wanted to feed his cats," I said. "Maybe even take 'em home with me in case it gets too cold. What're you still doin' here?"

"Same thing," he said.

"Really?"

"Not literally," he said. "When it snows or gets real cold I let Reuben Jefferson Jackson sleep in the back room."

"He's in there now?" I asked. "Not in back, not in the woods?"

"Yeah. I was just checking on him. I live within walkin' distance. I've got a key to Lonnie's shop for emergencies. I can let you in."

"That would be great," I said. "But I hate for you to wait. Can I borrow the key and give it back to you tomorrow?"

"I know what you're doin'," he said.

"You do?"

"You're gonna pick out some movies to ride out the storm with," he said. "I did the same thing earlier. Sure man. No worries."

"Thanks."

"I just hope Lonnie won't be off the wagon for long."

"Me too."

He removed the key from his ring, asked me to make sure it was the right one, then crossed the street and disappeared into the darkness on the other side.

Chapter Forty-eight

The shop was warm and dim. The only illumination came from a single nightlight behind the counter.

From some unseen place in the semidarkness, Shaft and Foxy Brown purred contentedly.

Quickly making my way over to the counter, I grabbed the small metal index card box, moved closer to the nightlight, and began flipping through the cards with the membership information on them.

It didn't take long.

All the victims and their moms were members.

Another confirmation. How many do you need before you get truly bold?

I think that was it.

I returned the box to its spot beneath the counter and started to walk out when a still-drunk Lonnie pressed the barrel of a revolver to the back of my head and cocked the trigger.

"Son a bitch think you gonna loot me . . . not during this or any other storm."

"Lonnie," I said. "It's me."

"John? John, what're you doin' here?" he said, stumbling across the words and pulling back the gun.

"Came to check on your cats," I said. "Thought you

were passed out somewhere sleeping it off."

"You're not here to rob me?"

"I'm not," I said. "I may take a movie, but I'll bring it back. And I'll pay for it."

"You don't have to pay me anything for it, buddy, no sirree."

"Thanks man."

"What were you doin' in my membership box?"

"Huh?"

"What were you doin' in my membership box?"

I drew a blank.

"Ah, oh . . . seein' if you had an address for Margaret's niece Susan," I said.

"Shouldn't you be lookin' for little Kenny Pollard instead of tryin' to dip your wick?"

"You're right," I said. "I should."

"'Less that's what you're really doing here," he said, suddenly sober. "How'd you know?"

"Know what?"

"Playtime's over, John. Tell me what you know. It's just us. The whole city's shut down. And I've got a gun. How'd you figure it out."

"Sobriety," I said.

"Sobriety?"

"Yeah. I've used the principles of AA and the Serenity Prayer a few times recently to help with things other than alcohol."

"Yeah?"

"Made me realize someone could use them to quit something other than drinking—like compulsive killing, say. I remembered your sobriety happened around the time Cedric disappeared—which was the time the killings stopped. What happened to Cedric sobered you

up, changed you. It was your moment of clarity that led
to sobriety. You were able to stay sober, to stop killing by
using AA."

"Was until you started stirring all this shit up again.
Compulsive is right. I'm not a bad man. I'm not some kind
of monster. I'm a man—a man like every other man, with
two wolves inside him. You've heard the old Cherokee
legend of the wolves, haven't you?"

Everybody has, I thought, *but if it keeps you talking, if it
gives me time to figure out what to do . . .*

"One evening an old Cherokee man told his
grandson about the war that wages inside all souls. The
battle is between two wolves, he told him. One wolf is
anger, envy, jealousy, sorrow, regret, greed, arrogance,
self-pity, guilt, resentment, inferiority, lies, false pride,
superiority, ego, even evil. The other is goodness, joy,
peace, love, hope, serenity, humility, kindness, benevolence,
empathy, generosity, truth, compassion, faith, even God."

He paused but I only nodded encouragingly.

"The boy thought about it for a while, then asked,
What determines which wolf wins? The old man simply
replied, The one you feed. I've been feeding the good wolf
since Cedric disappeared. I have a compulsion, but I've
been controlling it with the Twelve Steps."

"Tonight I remembered you drinking this afternoon
and how that coincided with Kenny's disappearance. At
first I had thought the killer might have gone to prison for
another crime or moved and was committing the murders
somewhere else, then it occurred to me you might be using
AA in the way I was."

"Don't ever let anyone tell you AA doesn't work," he
said. "It works." He then added with a demented smile, "If
you work it. Or until you stop working it. Think about what

I did. I stopped. I used AA to stop killing. Has anyone else ever done that? Ever? And I couldn't tell anybody. I knew something that could change the world, but had to keep it to myself."

"I kept asking who or where Cedric was running to," I said. "But when I turned it around and asked who or what he could be running from, I had to go back to where he was going in the first place. Here. To you. He was running from what he saw you doing."

"Guess he was, but I never saw him. Didn't know he had even come in. Thought I had the door locked. And maybe I did. He sometimes snuck in the back. When I realized he had been here, that this was the last place he had been before he vanished . . . it brought me up short."

I nodded.

"What it is you think he saw?" he asked.

"You raping or killing the final victim, Jaquez Anderson," I said. "My guess is your little meeting room back there wasn't just an adult room, but your playroom where you raped and killed and what? Recorded? Did you make videos of the boys? Did you rent them?"

"I never raped anyone," he said. "I'm a . . . I have a compulsion to kill, sure enough, but I never forced myself on anyone. I paid them boys to let me touch and film 'em, and to touch and do sex stuff to me, but I never forced 'em."

"That's a distinction without a difference," I said. "The very kind of stinking thinking AA deals with."

"And it did. Right up until you forced your way into my life and kicked the shit out of my serenity. Don't you get it? I stopped. I used the program to stop myself. I worked the shit out of it and was able to stop—until you had to dredge it all back up."

"Always someone else's fault," I said. "Big part of

that same mentality."

"You act like you know somethin', for some punk kid who just started the program."

"I don't know anything," I said. "Except where Cedric is."

I knew that really meant something to him.

"Do you? You do, don't you? You son of a bitch."

"How'd you lure Kenny?" I asked. "Comics?"

"And coloring books. Easiest thing in the world. Find a boy without a father. Thing he wants most in the world is some mature masculine attention. Where is Cedric?"

"Where is Kenny?"

"Where are any of the boys?" he said.

"In your walls," I said.

"How the hell did you—"

"That was something else that coincided with your sobriety and Cedric's disappearance. Your remodeling of your back room."

"Been tryin' to figure out what to do with them when I shut the place down," he said. "Couldn't come up with anything that didn't involve me gettin' caught."

"And why keep cats around when you're allergic to them?" I said. "Because you use the kitty litter on the bodies. It has a desiccant and odor-absorbing agent—and you can buy it in bulk without looking suspicious. But it would be suspicious if you didn't have cats. So you have Shaft and Foxy Brown and sneeze your way through every day and have bags and bags of kitty litter in your storage-meeting-burial chamber room. Wayne Williams reminded me that John Wayne Gacy hid his victims in the walls and floors of his house. Is Kenny already in there? Is that what you've been doing?"

"I'll tell you what I been doin', boy," he said. "I've been battlin' with demons you couldn't begin to understand, to keep from so much as touching that boy. Two wolves wagin' war inside me the likes of which you couldn't imagine. That's it. Worse thing I did to him so far is drug his Kool-Aid so he fell asleep before he got to finish his first comic. That's it."

"Let that be it," I said.

He laughed. "And what? Turn myself in? I've already done more than what any prison could do. I rehabilitated myself. I used the only program known to work for addiction and I stopped my addiction. Whatta they gonna do for me? Cage me? What's that gonna do? No, sir. I don't think so. Think instead I'll set you up for what's about to befall Kenny."

"By planting some of his clothes and comics in my apartment or car?"

"That was a nice touch," he said, "but an unnecessary one. Cops didn't care. Especially when they's havin' a new body every week. Missin' ain't murder. Missin' don't make it into the paper. Missin' don't come with no political pressure. Biggest mistake Wayne ever made was dumping them bodies."

"Let me see Kenny," I said.

"Let me see your brain," he said, holding up the gun a little higher. "It's pretty impressive. I want to see it."

"Did you kill Laney Mitchell?"

"Laney Mitchell? Now I'm a hit-and-run killer too?"

"Thought she might have seen something or found out something and had to be silenced."

He shook his head. "Sure it was just some drunk. Like you and me. Didn't mean no harm. Didn't stop him from doin' plenty, though, did it? Okay. Time to die."

"Wait. I know you want to know what happened

to Cedric," I said. "I know you want to see him. Let me
see Kenny. Let me take Kenny home and you can go see
Cedric."

"No way he's alive," he said.

"He's very much alive," I said. "I swear it. I'm telling
the truth. Put it to the test."

That reminded me of Lonnie passing a polygraph
in relation to Cedric's disappearance. Of course he did. He
had nothing to do with it. Had he been asked about the
other boys, that would've yielded a very different result.

"How?"

"You can ask who helped take him," I said. "She's
close by."

"She?"

A jingle at the door then—someone opening it,
triggering the bell—Lonnie's attention momentarily
diverted. Me lunging, grabbing, falling.

We hit the ground, the gun between us, both of us
vying for control over where the barrel was pointed.

Then Susan there. Spraying him with mace. Him
releasing his grip, pawing at his eyes. Me grabbing the gun.
Jumping up. Pulling her back out from behind the counter.

"Check the back room," I said to her.

As she did, I pointed the revolver at Lonnie and
blocked his exit from behind the counter. Not that he
was trying to exit. He was still rolling around on the floor
writhing in pain, spitting, crying, coughing, choking.

"It's empty," she said.

"Are you sure?"

Light from the room spilled out into the hallway.

"Positive."

"Check the bathroom."

She did.

"He's here," she yelled. "He's alive. Seems okay. Just

sleeping I think. John, he's alive. He's okay."

Chapter Forty-nine

"**W**hat're you doing here?" I asked Susan.

"I felt bad for all the pressure I had put on you. I was going to come to your apartment to surprise you and see if I could help."

We were waiting for the police to arrive.

Lonnie was still lying on the floor, but now he was crying, appearing to literally be wallowing. His self-pity was as pathetic as it was predictable.

"I had just finished cleaning and locking up," she said. "Already had my mace out. Saw Rand crossing Memorial and you come in here. Decided to take a look. I was feeling paranoid."

"Glad you were. Best surprise in a long time. Thank you."

"Did you really find Cedric?" Lonnie asked between snobs and sniffles.

"He didn't kill Cedric too?" Susan said.

"Just the others."

"Where are the bodies?"

"In the walls of the back room," I said.

"Oh my God. Right in there? Where you sent me to look for Kenny?"

"I didn't send you into the walls."

"Still."

"Did you really find him? Is he okay?" Lonnie said.
I nodded. "I think so."

"Where is he? Who took him?"

"I haven't decided whether or not I'm telling anyone," I said, "but I'm certainly not telling you."

With an inhuman growl, he lunged at me.

Unable to shoot him, I hesitated just long enough for him to be on me, tackling me to the ground, the gun falling out of my hand and skittering across the floor, disappearing beneath a video shelf.

Susan screamed.

Lonnie began beating me about the face, neck, and shoulders, his tears and snot falling down on me as he did.

Susan went for the gun, running past us, momentarily drawing Lonnie's attention.

I bucked him up off me and kicked him hard with both feet.

He went sailing back toward the back room, flailing as he did, and crashed into the large bookcases holding the thousands of video tapes in their hard plastic cases.

The shelves fell over, Lonnie following behind on his back, and knocked a hole in the sheetrock wall behind them, a hole out of which dropped a small, ashen, mummified hand along with a rain of white sheetrock dust, paper particles, and kitty litter.

Eventually, the cops came, Bobby Battle and Remy Boss among them.

"Looks like we owe you an apology," Remy said as Lonnie was being taken away.

"And that's the extent of it right there," Bobby said.

"So enjoy it. And don't be a dick about it."

A crime scene tech had already begun to open the walls behind the shelves and movie posters in the back room.

We had moved to the front of the store to be as far away from it as possible. I had no desire to see any more of the mummified murder of innocence I would never be able to unsee. The hand and all my imaginings were enough, were too much. Susan seemed to feel the same way.

"I have one favor to ask," I said.

"You and your goddamn favors," Bobby said.

"It's just because I'm young and have no authority and can't do them for myself. If I could, I'd never ask for anything. Believe that."

"I'll be glad when Frank is better and can get back to doin' them for you himself. He woke up a few minutes ago, by the way. He's gonna be okay."

Tears stung my eyes. "Thank God."

"What's the favor?"

"Let me and Susan take Kenny back to his mom."

"Seems the least we can do," Remy said.

"Which is what we try to do when we can," Bobby said. "He'll have to be taken to the hospital and checked out right after, but you can take him to the mom first."

"Thanks."

Camille Pollard burst into tears the moment she opened her door and saw us.

Her hair wasn't fixed. Her casual, comfortable clothes were worn and faded, and the light skin of her face held no makeup. It was the first time I had ever seen her not fixed up, not stylish, not made up, and she looked more youthful and more attractive than she ever had previously.

"Is he . . ."

"Just sleeping," I said.

Lights from the cop car that had brought us over flashed on the door and walls and still-falling snow.

I added, "They're going to take him to the hospital to check him out, but he's gonna be fine. An ambulance will be here in a minute."

I handed him to her.

As soon as I did, Wilbur pushed past her and hugged me.

I bent down and hugged him back.

"Where was he?" Camille said. "Who had him?"

I told her.

"Oh my God. Are you sure? Right next door all this time. Is he the . . . Did he kill the others?"

I nodded.

From the building across the way I could see Annie Mae Dozier open her door and look out at us.

"I actually was beginning to think it might be Mickey," she said. "Thought he might be doing this for his damn story. Where is he?"

"McDonough. He's fine. Was looking for Cedric. Now he's just waiting until the storm passes and the roads open again."

An ambulance pulled up.

"Come on," she said to Wilbur. "Let's get your brother to the hospital."

Chapter Fifty

Over the next several days, I spent a lot of time prayerfully pondering what I should do about Cedric. Turn over what I knew to the authorities in an attempt to find him and bring him home, or leave him where he was?

I didn't feel adequate to the task of deciding the fate of this little boy who had been through so much. I wasn't adult enough, mature enough, wise enough.

Who was I to say what was right or best for this child?

And yet . . .

Fate had made the decision mine to make, and Mickey had agreed to go along with whatever I decided.

Was he better off where he was or back with his mother?

I didn't want to decide, but more than that I didn't want to abdicate the responsibility I had been given.

In one sense, Annie Mae Dozier and her daughter were criminals—kidnappers who had stolen a child. In another, they were two caring women who had acted heroically in an attempt to save an abused and neglected child. Who knows, maybe the actions they took ensured that another isolated and traumatized child wouldn't turn to dark fantasies that would lead to much darker actions.

I realized I didn't have enough information to make the best decision possible, which let me know what I needed to do.

I went back to Annie Mae Dozier's.

"Figure I see you again," she said through her open door. "Heard you caught the killer. Tol' you that family was no good for Cedric."

I nodded.

"Why you here?"

"Trying to decide what to do," I said.

"'Bout?"

"Cedric."

"Leave the boy be."

"I'm inclined to," I said. "And I think you should be with them too."

Tears filled the old eyes behind the big glasses, and she stopped blinking.

Suddenly, this ancient, freckled, narrow, emaciated, parchment-covered thing before me was younger, more vibrant, and bent over no more.

"Y'all can be together," I said. "No running. No looking over your shoulder. All I want to do is talk with Cedric and your daughter. That's it. I have to make sure he's good before I can let it go. If you agree and he is doing well, no one will ever know and I'll be out of it forever. If you don't, I'll be forced to go to the authorities and . . . your daughter can be found. It wouldn't even be that difficult. You know it's true."

She nodded. "I do. Know somethin' else true too. That boy couldn't be any better or any happier. You'll see."

And I did.

And that was that. And like Kenny, a positive result was achieved for Cedric—something far too infrequent in what had become my work.

Susan and I started dating a little later. She had saved my life after all. It seemed the thing to do.

I still missed Jordan and I still felt conflicted about it.

I still missed Martin and I felt no conflict about that.

I stopped going to the missing and murdered children group. I never saw most of the members again, including Summer, who seemed more like a specter than anything else. Miss Ida and I stayed in touch. We had shared too much not to. Most often we'd meet at Jordan's grave.

I never found any evidence that Laney Mitchell's death was anything but a tragic, senseless, preventable accident. Maybe Lonnie was right. Maybe it was just a sad, sorry drunk like us.

Mickey continued calling and coming around while he was working on his book, but not much after that.

Frank got out of the hospital and made a full recovery. He continued to be the person in Atlanta I could count on most.

Two people who never got out of the hospital were Daryl Lee Gibbons and his mother—his mother because she died after a little less than a week inside and Daryl Lee because, when he was eventually able, he was sent straight from the medical hospital to a psychiatric one.

In the end, Martin's mother dropped her lawsuit for the most unexpected reason imaginable. Bobby Battle told her if she didn't he was going to arrest her for killing her own son and a hundred other charges besides, and that he could make them stick. She must have believed him. I never heard anything out of her again.

I found a new AA group and continued going. I

stopped drinking.

I got back in school—the first day back after the snowstorm in fact, and dug in to theology and my studies in a way I hadn't before.

And the reason I was able to do all this was because I was able to make a certain imperfect peace with the Atlanta Child Murders.

There were things I would never know and I was learning to live with that.

Were the victims connected? Yes. Many of them were intimately connected. Were there geographical and social relationships between victims and suspects? There were. Many.

Was there a child sex ring and more than one killer? I believe so.

I suspect John David Wilcoxen, Jamie Brooks, and others of all manner of evil—including murder of one kind or another—but because of the nature of such cases and the mistakes made by the various law enforcement agencies involved, there is much we will never know or be able to prove.

I believe that poor, at-risk, vulnerable street kids— the type of kids Wayne Williams called *drop shots*—were crushed by those streets and the predators lurking on them. I believe some kids sold their bodies and certain sexual services for money and attention and affection. I believe others were just available prey, children whose ancestry and geography sealed an impossibly cruel fate for them.

When people learn of my fascination with and investigation into the cases, they always ask me the same questions. Is Wayne Williams guilty? Did he do it?

It has taken a while, but I finally have an answer.

I believe Wayne Bertram Williams is the Atlanta Child Murderer. I still have many questions, but I am convinced by the evidence against him. There's simply too much of it, particularly trace evidence—the combination of fibers and human and dog hairs too unique, the probabilities against it being him too low—for it not to be Williams.

Wayne Williams also failed a polygraph three times.

But it's not just all of that. It's that he had such a ridiculous story about why he was on the James Jackson Parkway bridge the night he was stopped, or that the person he claimed to be looking for never came forward, or that he burned evidence, or that he had so many connections to so many of the key places, people, and victims, or that eyewitnesses claimed to have seen him with some of the victims, or that the relatively rare trilobal green carpet fibers from his bedroom as well as nearly twenty other fibers and hairs from his home and vehicle were found on so many of the victims, or that he used Cap'n Peg's as the address on his flyers, or that his flyers turned up in so many of the areas where the victims lived and were taken. It was Williams himself.

I don't believe Williams. I don't buy his explanations and find his protestations incredible.

That said, I don't believe he's responsible for killing everyone on the task force's list. I don't think it very likely he killed Clifford Jones, for example—or the two female victims, Angel Lenair and LaTonya Wilson. Or some of the others. And the blood of each and every one still cries out—for justice, for acknowledgment, for truth.

I believe Wayne Williams is a practiced and habitual liar. In short, I believe him to be a compulsive, sociopathic serial killer.

Partly because of the way the investigation was conducted, partly because of the nature of such cases, there are truths and facts about the cases we'll never know. Crimes will remain unsolved. Guilty people will remain free—or at least free from answering for these particular crimes.

Am I okay with that?

Do I have a choice?

About the Author

Multi-award-winning novelist Michael Lister is a native Floridian best known for literary suspense thrillers and mysteries.

The Florida Book Review says that "Vintage Michael Lister is poetic prose, exquisitely set scenes, characters who are damaged and faulty," and Michael Koryta says, "If you like crime writing with depth, suspense, and sterling prose, you should be reading Michael Lister," while Publisher's Weekly adds, "Lister's hard-edged prose ranks with the best of contemporary noir fiction."

Michael grew up in North Florida near the Gulf of Mexico and the Apalachicola River in a small town world famous for tupelo honey.

Truly a regional writer, North Florida is his beat.

In the early 90s, Michael became the youngest chaplain within the Florida Department of Corrections. For nearly a decade, he served as a contract, staff, then senior chaplain at three different facilities in the Panhandle of Florida—a unique experience that led to his first novel, 1997's critically acclaimed, POWER IN THE BLOOD. It was the first in a series of popular and celebrated novels featuring ex-cop turned prison chaplain, John Jordan. Of the John Jordan series, Michael Connelly says, "Michael Lister may be the author of the most unique series running in mystery fiction. It crackles with tension and authenticity," while Julia Spencer-Fleming adds, "Michael Lister writes one of the most ambitious and unusual crime fiction series going. See what crime fiction is capable of."

Michael also writes historical hard-boiled thrillers, such as THE BIG GOODBYE, THE BIG BEYOND, THE BIG HELLO, THE BIG BOUT, THE BIG BLAST featuring Jimmy "Soldier" Riley, a PI in Panama City during World War II. Ace Atkins calls the "Soldier" series "tough and violent with snappy dialogue and great atmosphere . . . a suspenseful, romantic and historic ride."

Michael Lister won his first Florida Book Award for his literary novel DOUBLE EXPOSURE. His second Florida Book Award was for his fifth John Jordan novel BLOOD SACRIFICE.

His nonfiction books include the "Meaning" series: THE MEANING OF LIFE, MEANING EVERY MOMENT, and THE MEANING OF LIFE IN MOVIES.

Lister's latest literary thrillers include DOUBLE EXPOSURE, THUNDER BEACH, BURNT OFFERINGS, SEPARATION ANXIETY, and A CERTAIN RETRIBUTION.

Thank you for reading **BLOOD CRIES!**

And don't miss all the exciting John Jordan Mysteries in the **BLOOD** Series.

Be sure to visit www.MichaelLister.com for more about other John Jordan Mysteries and Michael Lister's other award-winning novels.

Join Michael Lister's Readers Group at www.MichaelLister.com to receive news, updates, special offers, and another book absolutely **FREE!**